Goodbye, Mr. spalding

JENNIFER ROBIN BARR

CALKINS CREEK
AN IMPRINT OF HIGHLIGHTS
Honesdale, Pennsylvania

Calkins Creek
An Imprint of Highlights
815 Church Street
Honesdale, Pennsylvania 18431
calkinscreekbooks.com
Printed in the United States of America

ISBN: 978-1-68437-178-5 (hc)
ISBN: 978-1-68437-623-0 (eBook)
Library of Congress Control Number: 2018955601

First edition
10 9 8 7 6 5 4 3 2 1

Design by Barbara Grzeslo
The text is set in Sabon.
The chapter numbers are set in Chauncey Deluxxe Bold

To Mom—

the best storyteller I know

Life's Little Rules

(The Original Rules)

1. Take responsibility for every area of your life.
2. Things always happen for a reason.
3. Say "please" and "thank you."
4. Look people in the eye.
5. Commit yourself to constant improvement.
6. Don't expect life to be fair.
7. Always accept an outstretched hand.
8. Time heals all wounds.
9. Treat others the way you want to be treated.
10. Count your blessings.

1

A screen should be built over the right field wall at Shibe Park in Philadelphia.
—J.G. Taylor Spink, *The Sporting News*, August 30, 1934

Jimmie Foxx is definitely dead. I can tell by the way his glassy eyes are staring at me through the fishbowl. Finally. Who knew it would take three years for one fish to die? That means three years since the Philadelphia Athletics have played in a World Series. It also means Rule #13: *Bury all dead family pets in Shibe Park for luck.*

I turn onto my back and stare at the hairline crack across the bedroom ceiling. I should be more upset, and I squeeze my eyes shut trying to find an ounce of sadness. Instead, I feel a charge of excitement as my lips curl into a smile. Every time I bury a pet fish at Shibe Park, the A's go to the World Series.

I sneak out of bed, tiptoe to my third-floor window, and gaze out at the vast baseball stadium across the street. Shibe Park looks deserted, except for a glaring spotlight under the left-field stands. I wonder if some worker left it

9

on by accident. No time to worry about that now.

I rub my face awake, try to smooth down the pile of shaggy brown hair on my head and look for my knickers, finding them rolled up in a ball in the corner of the room. I'll need Lola's help. We have to bury Jimmie Foxx behind first base, before the sun comes up.

The Sheridans live in the row house next door, so Lola's bedroom window is only a few feet from mine. I tug on our Bingle—the name we gave the cord that runs from her window to mine—and listen for the faint *ding-a-ling* from the bell attached to the other end. Rule #16: *Always meet on the roof when you hear the Bingle.*

I gently wrap Jimmie Foxx in a handkerchief, grab my bag, and climb through the hallway skylight and onto the flat roof, our designated meeting place. I look to my left and my right, scanning the rows of rooftops for signs of anyone who might see us at this late hour, especially the Polinski brothers. They are always causing trouble in the middle of the night.

Each roof has something unique that makes it stand out, like Ma's tomato plants or her famous flowerpots, but they all have one thing in common: a set of rooftop bleachers to watch major league baseball games.

Tonight, all the bleachers are empty.

Our view of the ball field is the best on the block, right in the middle of the street. We can see easily over the short right-field wall and take in each game like we paid for the best seat in the house. Tomorrow, the street, our roof, and this ballpark will be filled with fans watching our Philadelphia Athletics play the Boston Red Sox.

I love game days. I love the roar of the crowd, the bell of the Good Humor truck, and the smells of Red Hots' sausages, steaming peanuts, and lit cigars. But at times like this, when Shibe Park is quiet and seems like it's all mine, I think I like it even more.

"I'm sorry you're dead, Jimmie," I whisper to the fish, "but we can't lose any more games. When the A's start winning again and folks pay to sit on our roof to watch, I'll think of you."

I try to put the naysayers out of my head—the parents who put down manager Connie Mack and the way he sells off his best players, the sportswriters who say the real Jimmie Foxx is past his prime, and even the Polinski brothers, who make it their mission to bully anyone who roots for the A's instead of the Phillies, especially me. All I know tonight is that I've got a dead fish, and he is going to bring us luck.

"Jimmy Frank! It's nearly midnight!" Lola says in a loud whisper, scaring me half to death. Tucking her flour-sack nightgown into overalls, she walks from her flat roof to mine, talking quickly as she arrives. "What could possibly be so important? I was having the best dream. I was dressed like Amelia Earhart—with the goggles and the scarf and the whole bit. But instead of flying, I was picketing in front of the White House with Alice Paul, who was telling me . . ."

11

"Can you tell me about your dream later? Jimmie Foxx is dead." I point to the fish lying on the white handkerchief.

Lola's pale skin shines white in the darkness of the late night, and her long curly brown hair falls over her shoulder as she leans over to inspect it.

"Jimmy Frank killed Jimmie Foxx. Now *that's* a fun headline," she says. She knows I didn't kill him, and I choose to ignore her comment. We stand in silence, both gazing down.

"So I guess we'll need a burial," she finally says, "in the ground. Gram still talks about how Great Uncle Ronan probably isn't in Heaven because he wasn't put in the ground."

"Where was he put?"

"Nobody knows. He died in The Great War, somewhere in France or something."

"Maybe he is in the ground," I say, hopeful. Not going to Heaven seems awful. "That's why we're here, anyway. Rule #13."

"We haven't needed Rule #13 for a long time." Lola opens my bag, pulls out our thin book of rules, and reads: "Rule #13: *Bury all dead family pets in Shibe Park for luck.*"

"How about first base?" I point to the spot in the ballpark where the real Jimmie Foxx plays.

Lola looks at me with a tilt of her head and one

eyebrow raised. "Do you really think a dead fish is going to bring them luck?"

"All I know is that in each of the years I buried a pet fish somewhere in the park, they went to the World Series. It is *not* a coincidence." She lets me keep talking with that *here-we-go-again* look of hers. "Quit looking at me like that! Now that Jimmie Foxx is dead, we need to get moving." I make my way to the ladder at the back of the roof. "You coming?"

"Rule #13 or not, there is no way that team can climb out of the basement this year," she says, following me.

"But what happens if they win a few?"

"Well, *they win a few*. Whoop-de-do."

"No, listen. Maybe they win a few. And maybe, because of that, a few more people want to come out to watch a game. Then, *just maybe,* some of those folks decide to come up to *our* roof and pay money to *our* parents instead of going into the ballpark." Lola purses her lips. I know she cannot disagree with this.

"We can really use the money," she says, looking down at her shoes. "Ma says that starting next week, I'll have to pitch in at the shop right after school."

"Really?" is all I can muster to say. Our daily after-school trip to the playgrounds at Reyburn Park and the Funfield Rec Center might be coming to an end.

"Well, my parents can't really pay someone right now. I can tailor clothes just as good as anyone."

"When did you learn all that fancy stitching?"

"I didn't. But I can sew buttons and hem pants and skirts."

"So that's why we need to do this. If just one more person watches a game from our roof, that could be one less afternoon at the shop."

"I guess. Maybe."

"More than maybe!"

"Fiiiiine," she says with a half-smile, trying to sound like she's doing me a favor. But she and I both know that she was coming all along.

Rule #12: *Jimmy and Lola will always be best friends forever.*

2

Lola and I gather our things from the hiding spot under the front porch. Lola takes my Army Musette bag, the one Poppi gave me from The Great War. He had only one rule when he gave it to me—Rule #20: *Keep fishing line, a matchbook, a library card, and a canteen on your person at all times.* I don't use most of them, but I keep them in the bag anyway. You never know.

She stuffs the bag with all sorts of things we've stashed away over the years: a small shovel, a flashlight, a piece of parchment paper, a pencil, and of course, her writing journal.

"Here." I hand her a small piece of cloth and watch as she tucks Jimmie Foxx into a tin sardine box, just big enough for a fish-size coffin. With everything packed, we are ready to put our plan into action.

There are no cars, no lit streetlamps, and not a single

bit of trash on 20th Street. We all moved here for the ballpark, and our neighbors take pride in keeping this street clean. Tomorrow, there will be men in their dapper pinstripes and fedora hats jumping on the trollies, or walking up our street to see the game. Maybe one or two new folks will come up to our roof instead of buying a real ticket.

We stand on the sidewalk and look at the twelve-foot wall just across the street from our porches. A sudden squeak from old Mrs. Carson's screen door makes us both jump, and we duck in the shadow until we are sure she's inside. She is the eyes and ears of the neighborhood. She knows all the secrets.

It's chillier than I expect for the last day of August, and I take in a deep, cool breath before crossing.

We've always found ways to sneak into Shibe Park— propping open doors, prying back wooden fence panels, hiding in delivery trucks. Finally, now that we are almost thirteen years old, we are tall enough to sneak over the short right-field wall. We've learned how to scout the street for people and how to hide in the darkness, waiting for our chance.

It took some planning at first. One late April night, we dug two grooves in the wood: one about halfway up, and another a few feet above that. At the top of the wall, we nailed a small piece of rope. Lola got that idea from one of my *Boys' Life* magazines. Of course. She's always reading them more than me.

"Let's go," she says. "Squat down."

The plan is simple. When the street is clear, Lola goes over first. She steps first on whatever we can find on the street. It might be a cinder block left over from a kid's game of half-ball, or maybe a wooden crate that a food vendor forgot.

Lola steps from the crate onto my shoulder, her other foot finding the first small groove and her hand finding the next. She grabs the rope. I give her a big push, and she swings her leg over to sit on the top.

"Mmmph," she grunts.

"Shhh!"

"Oh, quit worrying. Nobody is around here!" she says, waving her hands and balancing as she sits, with one leg on each side of the wall. I still try to hurry.

I'm two inches taller than Lola, but I still need some help. I step on the crate, find the same two grooves and rope, and grab onto Lola's outstretched arm to launch the momentum to land on the top. We both quickly swing our legs over and drop to the other side.

The first couple of times we did this were tricky. A few falls and sore behinds reminded us for days. But we've had a summer of practice, and now we can make it over in thirty seconds flat. Tonight is just as easy.

We land in the warning track and squat down, dirt kicking up all around. The vast ballpark is deserted in front of us, but the spotlight underneath the left-field stands is still on.

"Lola," I nudge her and point.

"Somebody probably just left it on today," she says, breaking up my thoughts. "No need to worry."

"Sure," I say, my voice squeaking a bit.

"Besides, you've never worried before."

"I guess I never really thought about getting caught before." I step back to the shade of the outfield wall. "You think we'll lose Mr. Shibe's business at the hardware shop? Or maybe they won't give the uniform orders to your parents anymore? And what about being batboy next year? If we are caught sneaking in, and they realize who we are . . ."

"Jimmy," Lola looks me straight in the eye, "we've done this a million times, and you were the one who wanted to bury your fish. Come on." She puts her hand on my arm and softens her tone. "You can walk around this ballpark blindfolded and still escape without being seen."

She's right, as usual. We've been sneaking into Shibe Park for as long as I can remember. Most of the time, we play jacks or cards. Sometimes we just sit in the dugout or gaze up at the stars—nothing to cause alarm. But, for the first time, the image of getting caught sticks with me. A's manager Connie Mack has promised I can be batboy next year—a real job with steady money. I can't lose that. Almost every boy in my class at St. Columba wants it. Except for the Polinskis, of course. I can't imagine them ever having a real job.

We jog to first base and find the perfect spot for a burial, right where the real Jimmie Foxx stands.

"I think we should be careful about the dirt," Lola says, almost to herself. She slowly slides the shovel beneath the dry, brown infield, pulling up a rectangular-shaped piece and laying it to the side. She starts on the small hole as I unpack the bag.

"What's the paper for?" I ask.

"To write something down. Go ahead. We can bury him with it."

What do you say about a dead fish? Yes, he was named after my favorite ballplayer—an all-star who everyone respects, and one of the only good players left from our World Series streak a few years ago.

But this is about more than just our first baseman. It seems strange burying something dead to bring the team back to life. But it's worked before. It can work again.

The finger snap in front of my eyes wakes me from the daydream.

"Jimmy! One minute, you're shaking in your boots, and the next minute, you're lollygagging around!"

We both laugh a little as I start to write:

> Dear Jimmie Foxx,
> You were a good fish.
> I hope you go to Heaven.
> Love, Me

I would have liked to sign my actual name, but if this box is ever found, "James Martucci Frances III" will get me into some serious trouble. I place the note in the tin box and put it into the hole.

"Okay," she says. "You should say something."

"Something," I snort.

Lola muffles a laugh. "Jimmy, this *is* a funeral. Say something nice." She forces a somber tone. "Gram says that death leaves a heartache that no one can heal. You have to say goodbye."

"But I just wrote a note!"

Her eyes don't flinch.

"Fine."

I look down and stomp on the disturbed ground to flatten it once again. I talk fast. "You were named after the great Jimmie Foxx. He's a first baseman and bought me a cherry Coca-Cola over at Doc Hoffman's last summer. He even won Most Valuable Player a couple of times. I, ah, like how our names are similar. Please bring him luck. Please bring the team luck. Please help them win." I pause. "Oh, and if you see Lola's great uncle Ronan, tell him hello."

"Amen," we say together. I fling my bag across my chest, and we head toward our exit—through an employee door on the other side of the ballpark.

"Hey, that light just went out," Lola says, looking across to left field.

We lock eyes, both knowing what that means.

My feet are moving before I even realize it. We race across the field. Lola is faster than me, and she pulls my hand as we sprint.

We hop into the stands behind third base, run up the aisle, and hide in the stairwell.

"Stay here while I check to make sure the coast is clear," Lola whispers.

"Wait!" I try to grab her arm, but she's already gone. I stay still, and my eyes dart between the columns and back down the aisle to the field.

My breathing echoes throughout Shibe Park. Or is that just in my head?

The shadows are moving. Or are they?

I close my eyes and hold my breath. A bead of sweat slides down my face, and I strain to listen for the sound of someone walking. What if they find us? There goes batboy. There goes our freedom in the ballpark. There goes the family business.

Get a hold of yourself, Jimmy.

My eyes pop open at the tug on my shirt. Lola's grin washes away some of my fear, and she motions for me to follow. I don't think she'll ever be nervous.

We tiptoe toward the exit, sliding our backs against walls that seem to never end. We shuffle quietly until we find the door. I unlock it from the inside knob with a loud click, and we both freeze, listening for anyone that might be near us. Lola peeks outside to make sure Lehigh Avenue is empty, jumping back and holding the door closed.

21

Someone is walking near the entrance. We silently wait in the darkness.

Please hurry. My eyes have adjusted to the darkness, and I can see even Lola taking deep breaths.

Finally, the coast is clear. We slip through the door and shut it tight. I exhale as we sprint toward the corner.

We sneak in the shadows down 21st Street past the ticket booth, round the grandstand entrance, and turn at the front tower of Shibe Park onto Lehigh Avenue, around the corner from our houses. We stay close to the stadium wall, giggling nervously, and passing each engraved and arched window quickly.

I suddenly feel invincible and look up. From this side, I would never guess this is a major league ballpark. It looks more like a castle, or something I might find in Italy or France or some other place I have only read about in books. Lola's a step ahead and reaches back for my hand to help me catch up.

"You should have seen your face, Jimmy," Lola laughs, breaking the silence of the last ten minutes.

"I knew we'd make it out," I say, with as much confidence as I can muster. Why was I so nervous? We are safe, Jimmie Foxx is buried, and our luck is about to change.

"Well it's a good thing the Polinskis didn't see you shaking. They'd never let you live it down," she eggs me on.

"I wasn't shaking!" I give her a small shove. "Why do you always bring them up anyway?"

"Because one day you're going to stand up to them."

"Yeah, sure." I grin at the thought, knowing that one Polinski brother versus one Jimmy Frank is a lopsided fight. Four Polinskis is a massacre.

"I'm serious, Jimmy."

"No way. Nobody who has ever stood up to them has come out okay. You remember what happened to Matty and Ralph last year." Lola grimaces at the memory. Their faces were bruised for weeks.

"They are the worst kind of bullies," she says.

"What do you mean? Like there are good bullies?"

"I *mean*, they bully you one minute, and expect you to play with them the next."

"Well you can't play half-ball with four kids, so I guess they need us. I just keep my head down and out of their way. I'll play games when they want me to, and ignore them when they don't," I say. "Besides, that one Polinski seems a little different than the rest."

"Which one?"

"The youngest one. I think he's our age. I don't know his name," I say.

"The only name that matters is Polinski, Polinski, Polinski, Polinski." She counts them out on her fingers. "One Polinski is the same as the next. They're all bad."

"Even in school, Father Ryan calls them all Mr. Polinski," I say with a smirk.

She rolls her eyes and opens her mouth to reply when we both spot people sitting on my porch. We dive toward the row of homes, crouching out of sight.

"Did they see us?" she whispers.

"No. It looks like my parents, your dad, Mr. Donahue, and Mr. O'Connor."

"That's strange. Something must be wrong."

"Let's go under."

We squat down on the sidewalk out of their sight, peel back the side panel, and slip underneath the porch. We crouch quietly, trying to figure out what is happening to bring out the neighbors at this late hour.

"I'm surprised it isn't in the papers yet," Pop says.

"Aw, they're too busy covering that Detroit pitcher Schoolboy Rowe and his winning streak. This doesn't matter to them," Mr. O'Connor says. "All this here? This is just for spite. They are finally getting their way."

The men are talking in what seems like a riddle. Over the next few minutes, we strain to hear words like *lawsuit*, *ordinance,* and *municipality.* Mr. O'Connor keeps cursing a man named Dilworth. I look to Lola, but she shrugs. I point to my ear and inch closer to their voices.

"But it *will* be in the papers soon," Ma's breaks into the conversation. Normally cheerful, her voice is low and sad. "No more secret meetings in the middle of the night. We need to tell the kids." Lola and I lock eyes at the mention of kids.

"For spite or not, once this happens, there will be no more watching baseball from our rooftops. And gentlemen, there will be nothing we can do about it."

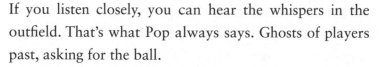

3

If you listen closely, you can hear the whispers in the outfield. That's what Pop always says. Ghosts of players past, asking for the ball.

I don't hear anything right now. The stadium is silent as a photograph. I walk to the mound and look toward home plate. I'm ready for anyone.

That's when I hear the voice.

"Jimmy," it says softly in the distance. I swing around and search the outfield.

"Jimmy," it whispers again, laughing at me.

"JIMMY FRANK!"

I jerk awake to a squeaking sound, a foul smell, and something soft and white covering my eyes.

Underpants.

"Nina! Cut it out!" I say, squinting and watching my sister collect the laundry across the room. She has opened the bedroom curtain and sunlight is blazing into my eyes.

"Snap to it, golden boy," she sneers. "It's not like *you* to oversleep on game day." My body shoots up and I dash out of bed. People will be arriving for the game in no time, and I still have to sweep off the roof.

I open the window and look across the street to Shibe Park. The ballpark activity is well under way. The groundskeepers are finishing up the infield lines and cleaning off the pitcher's mound. I'd know the squeaking sound of the line-marker wheels any day.

The street is loud with that game-day buzz. It's never as busy as it was a few years ago, but it's still where all the action happens.

There is a chill in the air this morning. It's been such a long, hot summer. Maybe the cooler day will bring the team back to life. Well, the cooler day and a dead fish.

"Jimmy Frank, come down here!" I look down to see the Polinski brothers putting together a game of half-ball. They need more kids for a full game and are waving for me to join. "Get down here. Now."

I shake my head. "Chores!" I yell down and slide just to the left of my window, out of their sight. I'm relieved to have a real excuse to avoid them today.

A honk grabs my attention. Clouds of dust and dirt surround two police officers on horseback who are trying to clear one last car, and the street is becoming more crowded each minute. There is a Red Hots' sausage cart setting up, and a few men in suits and hats are heading toward the ticket window. The smell of crisp Italian sausage makes its way to my nose, and my stomach grumbles.

I grab my knickers out of the laundry basket, put on my lucky A's cap, and fill my army bag with all the goodies I've collected for today's game. I have a special treat for Lola. I make my way into the hallway and climb up the ladder, through the skylight, and onto our rooftop.

I try not to think about the conversation we heard under the porch. Or the half-conversation we heard. Whatever they were talking about in the middle of the night makes me worry. But when I go through the skylight, all these thoughts are overcome by blue skies, bright sun, and a cool breeze perfect for baseball.

My pre-game chores are easy. I sweep the roof in no time, give Ma a peck on the cheek, and eat one of her famous roast-pork sandwiches for breakfast. Pop is wiping off the bleachers as Nina tries to convince him to let her miss the game and go to her friend Kate's house.

"No. You'll stay here and tend to our guests," he says, continuing to clean.

"*Maaaaaa*." Nina stomps away and Pop shakes his head.

"We have the best view in the city. How can you not love baseball?" he asks her, knowing the question will go unanswered. "I hope it'll be a big crowd today." Pop looks over to me.

"Sure thing, Pop," I reply. Nina is imitating me with

27

a silent and overexaggerated *Sure thing, Pop* behind him.

"It's a great day for a game." He slaps me on the back and looks up. "There is nothing like a baseball game on a sunny afternoon."

I give him a *you bet* nod. Ma squeezes my shoulder, and we all look over to the Shibe Park grounds. Neither of them seems upset. Maybe last night was nothing? Pop kisses her cheek and whispers something into her ear, which makes her smile. Ma has the best smile.

People are starting to arrive on our rooftop. Most are popping up through the skylight, but a few have made it all the way up from the back ladder that runs down all three stories to the ground.

"Hold up, Miss," I say, as one lady catches her dress on the top of the ladder. I take her hand and release the dress. Nina sticks her finger down her throat like she's going to throw up.

"You sure have a good kid here," Mr. Fletcher says, shaking my hand and looking across the street as the Shibe Park stands fill up. "Bet this view never gets old. Shibe is a fool if he takes this awa—"

"Good to see you, Fletch." Pop cuts him off and shakes his head just a little, as if to say "no."

The conversation from last night rushes back to me.

"Well," Mr. Fletcher replies, glancing quickly from Pop, to me, and back to Pop. "Say, did ya hear there was another break-in on 22nd Street? They hit two shops this time," he continues, awkwardly changing the subject.

"No, I didn't. I was at our store this morning. No break-in for us," Pop says.

"I bet it was those darn Polinski brothers again. You stayin' away from those boys?" Mr. Fletcher directs his question back to me.

"Um. Mostly, sir. But what exactly did you mean about . . ."

"Nothing but trouble, those Polinskis. Don't forget the '31 World Series," he continues. "Stole from your father's store. Money out of your own hands. And right there in the middle of game three."

He is going out of his way to stay on this subject, but no matter what he says, *Shibe is a fool if he takes this away* circles my thoughts.

"You should've never let them go." He turns back to Pop, who rolls his eyes.

"They were just little kids. Their father was in jail."

"Seems like he's always in jail. Teach 'em early. That's what I always say. Now they strut around here like they own the place."

"Yes, well . . ." Pop becomes lost in his own thoughts. Mr. Fletcher is right. Getting away with that break-in was when it all changed. They went from being neighborhood kids to neighborhood bullies. The worst part? They thought *I* snitched on them. And they've never let me forget it.

"I need to finish," I say, holding up the broom. They seem to have forgotten why Mr. Fletcher brought the

Polinskis up in the first place—to distract me. It didn't work, anyway. I need to tell Lola about what I just heard: *Old-man Shibe is a fool if he takes this away.*

"*Pssst,* Lola." I wave her over.

"What?"

"Mr. Fletcher just . . ." I whisper in her ear.

"Aw, aren't you two *cute!*" Nina interrupts, loud enough for everyone to look.

"You sure are grouchy today," Lola scoffs at her, but we quickly separate and avoid each other for a while.

I take twenty-five cents from each person and give it to Ma, who puts it into her front apron pocket. She smiles each time and loudly says across the rooftop, *Thank you, Mr. so-and-so.* I see her counting the money. With the sunny skies, a Sunday game, and Ma's food, I bet we can make ten dollars today. And with the way Ma can bargain, ten dollars will buy us food for more than a week.

I'm deep in my thoughts as the dugouts fill up with the Philadelphia Athletics and Boston Red Sox players. I need to shake off the distractions and find my seat. It's time for Rule #11: *Watch every single Philadelphia Athletics home game from our rooftop, no matter what.*

4

I make my way around the stands and take my spot on the front right corner edge of our bleachers. From here, I can see everything in the ballpark—every pitch, every fly ball, every run. It also lets me sit right next to Lola, who sits on the far left edge of her bleachers.

The stands behind us—ten elevated, wooden rows on top of our flat roof—are now filled with all kinds of folks chatting away. Random bits of conversation break through the noise:

... *six daughters and one on the way* ...

... *leaving town, heading back to Ireland* ...

... *textile workers are striking just before midnight* ...

... *the bank is taking their home* ...

Not one conversation is about baseball. What makes an adult come out to a ballpark and not concentrate on the game is a mystery to me. I try to put everything out of my mind and focus on the game.

It'll be strange to see Lefty Grove, the A's former all-star, playing against Jimmie Foxx and Bing Miller and all of the A's players I love. It's probably strange for him to play against his friends. But he left and took more money in the big player trade of '33, when Connie Mack signed away most of our key players to "rebuild" the team.

"Hogwash," Pop always says. "There's no rebuilding, Jimmy. If you ask me, all we got out of it was fewer folks on our roof buying seats and spending money."

Lola arrives and pulls out her journal. I watch her write "September 1, 1934" on the corner. She sees me looking, slams it shut, and gives me a "friendly" push forward that's hard enough to knock me right off my seat. I laugh until I realize the Polinski brothers were watching from the street and give a howl in my direction.

"Geez, Lola! Why can't you be more like other girls?" I snap. She scowls at me with her squinty eyes. I quickly look away and rummage through the bag to make sure nothing has fallen out. I can feel my face grow redder and redder, until Lola finally gives in and cracks a smile. Her face lights up. Sometimes, I don't know if I want her to be more like a boy or more like a girl.

"Alright, Jimmy Frank, let's see what you got today," she says.

I sit down and pull the bag from over my shoulder. I carefully pull out each item, placing them on our legs.

"One box of candy cigarettes. A bag of boiled peanuts."

She's pretending to fall asleep at my slow reveal, which makes me draw the process out even longer.

"Two licorice sticks. One Peanut Chews."

Behind us, I place two black-cherry pops, our book of rules, and my lucky baseball, the first home run ball I ever caught. The bat must have hit the ball smack in the middle, because I can only make out the S and the G from the word *Spalding* written across the center.

I also take out the canteen of water and the latest issue of the *Saturday Evening Post* that came in yesterday's mail. She sees that and grabs it.

"Well?" I say. Today was my day to bring the snacks, a rule we added last April when the A's finally started playing on Sundays. Rule #23: *Take turns bringing snacks to Sunday games*. I've been collecting them for two weeks.

"Not bad," she says casually. I know she's impressed, by the way her lips are curling up at each end.

I save the best for last.

"And one pack of Valomilk." I take the orange and brown wrapped candy out of the bag and place it on Lola's leg.

"Not bad at all." She rips it open and bites, as gooey marshmallow oozes out. "Where'd you get the money for all this?"

"I've been making deliveries for the pharmacy on 22nd street. Ten cents a run."

"Why didn't you tell me?"

"To surprise you," I say quietly so that Nina can't hear me. "You know when I'm batboy next year, I won't be able to watch the games with you." My cheeks flush a little, and she doesn't say anything at first. Her eyes are still looking ahead, and her lips are pursed shut.

"Yes, well, I'll be too busy anyway," she finally says. "Doing something important, like writing for *The Bulletin* or advising President Roosevelt, or running my own ball club, *for girls*."

"I don't doubt it," I say without kidding around. "I really just wish you could come with me. You know, like as a bat girl."

Lola looks directly at me.

"Jimmy Frank! Do you think the great and powerful *Connie Mack* could ever possibly allow a girl into the dugout?"

"It's just a wish, Lola," I say. "And besides, why not? I mean, there's got to be some baseball owners that are girls."

"Women," Lola corrects me. "Don't worry, Jimmy. I'll break some sort of barrier one day. I just don't think it will be as bat girl for the A's."

Ralph and Matty, the twins from 24th Street, jump on either side of us. The rest of our bottom row is empty, but the stands behind us have filled up nicely. I glance back— there must be twenty people here.

"It's game day!" Matty says, with his permanent

34

goofy grin. They start to grab for the snacks, and Lola swats at their hands. I quickly shove everything back into my bag.

"Where's Santa?" I ask. Stanley St. Nick lives near Ralph and Matty on 24th Street. The three of them are always together.

"Pa said they were packing up their store today," Ralph replies.

"So, that's really happening." I slump back on the bench.

"Yep. Their rent is too high," Lola says. "You know it's double on a corner."

"Where am I gonna buy my baseball cards?" Matty asks. Lola shoots him a look, and he shrinks a little.

"Pa said Mr. St. Nick was down at the dock in Fishtown looking for some work," Ralph says. "And he's gonna try the Tastykake factory. They're looking for wagon drivers."

"Hey! Santa can sneak us free snack cakes," Matty adds. Lola promptly smacks the back of his head.

"But those factory jobs fill quick. Besides, that's all the way down in Hunting Park," I say.

"At least it's in the city. It's better than moving," Ralph says.

"Moving?"

"They have family in Brooklyn," Matty adds. "Maybe they'll move to New York."

"Or go back to Ireland," Lola says.

We become silent, worry slowly washing over all of us. We've heard these stories before, but this is one of us. It feels closer, and I look at my friends. It's Santa today, but it could be any of us tomorrow.

5

For the first time in my life, it's hard to concentrate on the game. I try to tune out all my worries. We watch the players make their way out to the field.

Lola stretches behind me and takes her journal, a tattered book filled and filled and *filled* with words on the front and back of each page. I think it's a combination of diary entries, short stories, and pretend newspaper articles. She says she's going to be a publisher, or a novelist, or another Sarah Hale, whatever that means. She's always throwing around names of important women that I don't know.

A lot of what she writes is her "private stuff," and I better not look or she'll pop me one. But every so often she writes something and reads it aloud. It's always funny and makes me laugh. I wish she would do it more often.

"Lefty Grove returns to face sulking A's," she says out loud as she writes.

Down in the ballpark, folks have filed into their seats. "It's a sea of hats," Lola mumbles to herself, still writing. She's right. It is a sea of men's top hats, ladies' brimmed hats, and kids' ball caps. The stands are filled today, unusual for a game at the end of a miserable season.

But today's game has it all—a cool fall breeze breaking through the crisp summer sun, and a town favorite now playing for a rival team. I guess if you put all the right things together, even in a bad season, folks will come out to watch.

"Jimmy, after the second inning, go on down for another tray of pork sandwiches," Ma says quickly as she passes, "and don't forget to bring one over to Mrs. Carson."

"Sure thing, Ma." I look back and I see she has stopped. She walks back toward us with a strange look on her face.

"Have I told you how much I love you today?" She kneels down and grabs each side of my face.

"Ma, *stop*!" I urgently whisper. Ralph and Matty are trying to hold in their laughter.

"Well," she stands up and gathers herself, "I want to make sure you all enjoy the game. Don't do any customer runs, okay? No distractions—really watch it." She looks out toward the game. "What a view."

"But Ma, the school fair is later." She looks back at

me, and confusion washes across her face. I never mind running down to the street carts for food, or cigars, or iced tea, or whatever the folks in our stands need. Carl at the Red Hots' stand sometimes gives me an extra sausage on a bun, and Hal at the hot pretzel cart always slides a second one into the bag.

"Money," Lola interjects. "He wants to make money for the fair."

"She's right. I can make fifty cents on runs today. *Please?*"

"We'll see," she says. But I already know she warned her customers not to bother me.

"She's acting strange," Lola whispers after Ma leaves.

"They all are. Right before the game, Mr. Fletcher said *Shibe is a fool if he takes this away.*"

"What in the world does that mean?"

"I have no idea."

"Maybe he's finally moving the team to Jersey," Matty chimes in, and Ralph punches his arm. "Quit it! You know they've been talking about that for years. Right over to Camden."

"They've been talking about *a lot* of things for years," Ralph says. "Nothing ever happens."

"It sounds bad. Whatever it is . . ." Lola mutters and starts to scribble in her notebook. I stare ahead as the game gets under way.

Both teams come out swinging. We score twice in the first inning, only to have the Red Sox answer with four

39

runs of their own. Even down two runs, I am happy for the distraction.

But scoreless innings follow and the energy fades.

Ralph and Matty are playing jacks and talking about last night's radio episode of *The Lone Ranger*. Lola is reading my copy of *The Saturday Evening Post*, glancing up every so often. By the end of the fifth inning, the adults have picked up their conversations from earlier. Pop and I are the only ones really paying attention. Things don't change until the sixth inning, when Eric McNair hits a home run to deep left field.

"Atta boy!" Pop yells. Everyone looks back to the game. It suddenly becomes interesting again. By the ninth inning, the A's have ten hits and are trailing by one run. Lefty Grove has come in to pitch for Boston.

"Lefty looks old," I say to Lola, purposely loud enough for Pop to hear me.

"You're right about that!" Pop chimes in. "You'll see, Jimmy, we'll take advantage of him right now."

Pop is right. In no time, there is a runner on second base and one out. A long single here will tie the game. A home run will win it. I can't help but think about our fish burial. Now we need some luck.

Jimmie Foxx is coming to the plate. He walks slowly, kicks the dirt off his shoes, and spits toward the dugout. And then he stares down his old friend Lefty Grove— with a long, hard, steady stare.

Lefty is not only older but also slow as molasses. He takes long, deep breaths in between every pitch. He looks at second base, stretches his arms up, and then throws one right down the middle.

A perfect pitch.

A pitch to hit.

Strike one.

"You know how this is going to end," Lola says. I don't look at her. I know what she is going to say. Jimmie Foxx is going to work a full count, keeping us on our toes and excited. He may even hit a few long foul balls to get the crowd going. But in the end, he'll strike out. It's just how the season is going, lucky dead fish or not.

But she's wrong.

The next pitch looks the same at first, but this time, Foxx swings. I grab Lola's arm as his bat hits the ball. All the spectators gasp as the *Crack!* echoes off the stadium walls like a gunshot. His bat splits in two, and Lefty Grove dives out of the way as wooden bat shards shoot toward the pitching mound. There's no way this ball is going far with a broken bat. It's probably a foul ball, as predicted.

But the folks in the stands are looking toward us in right field. That ball is still flying, its arc high as it quickly starts downward. Closer to us. We all hold our breath.

Mr. Harvey is on his roof screaming, "Come on! Come on!" Down in the street, a group of kids are running behind the twelve-foot right-field wall, hoping to catch a home run. The people in the ballpark shield their eyes from the sun.

Down. Down. Down.

And over.

"GOODBYE, MR. SPALDING!" Pop yells as the baseball just clears our short wall in right field—the short wall that allows us to watch every game from our very own rooftop. The short wall that Lola and I sneak over all the time to hang out in the ballpark or bury dead fish. The best home run wall in all of baseball.

The stands erupt with waving arms and hats. Pop is shaking hands with every person on our bleachers. Nina even cracks a smile. Kids are diving for the ball as it bounces off of 20th Street, and the great Jimmie Foxx is rounding the bases. His teammates rush the field, patting him on his back as he runs home. I hug Lola, and I don't care if anyone sees.

A Jimmie Foxx home run wins the game.

And we had something to do with it.

6

"Best Shibe Park memory ever?" Lola asks a few minutes later, as she scribbles in her journal. Ralph and Matty have headed home to grab dinner before the fair. I'm still staring at the field.

"One of them." I shrug my shoulders. "There are too many to pick just one." I start rattling off other Shibe Park memories. Great plays made in the field by Lou Gehrig or Ty Cobb. Long home runs that we watched bounce off a rooftop to a collection of waiting kids below.

Lola continues to write as I describe the crisp October day when right-fielder Bing Miller looked up to me and gave me a wave and a big goofy grin.

"And don't you know, he hit a double right off the scoreboard to win the game that day!" I continue, now realizing that most of the remaining folks on the rooftop are listening.

"It sure is something special," Mr. Fletcher says, looking across the street. "It will indeed be a sad day when they block this view."

I crinkle my forehead, and Lola stops in her tracks.

"I think it's time you tell him," he says to Pop. They shake hands as everyone says their goodbyes and makes their way down.

Ma lingers in the corner. Pop looks nervous.

"What?" I ask. Ten more questions come out of my mouth before Lola sits next to me and squeezes my arm to tell me to stop. We exchange worried looks as Ma and Pop wave for Mr. Sheridan to come from his roof to ours.

"You want to tell them, Jack?" Pop looks at Lola's father, who shakes his head.

"Nah, it's all yours."

Ma comes over and holds Pop's hand, taking over. "It looks like they are going to build a wall—one that is tall enough to block our view," she says.

The news hits me slowly, like they are talking through some sort of tunnel. I look toward Shibe Park.

I see the grooves and rope that Lola and I use to sneak in. *That's got to be one big wall,* I think to myself. It's hard to even picture. My mind wanders to the last time I saw Babe Ruth, a few weeks ago. I can swear he looked toward my roof and nodded his head.

Lola nudges me, and I snap back to Pop, who is now talking. Lola is writing fast, and Ma sits next to me. Nina is standing near the corner with her arms crossed. Even she looks white as a ghost.

"I can't sit through this again," she says and goes down the skylight.

"Again? Does Nina already know? Does everyone?" I bark.

"We told Nina this morning. She'll have to . . ."

"Jimmy, remember The Rules," Ma cuts Pop off and gently rubs my back. Of course, she's not talking about *my* rules. She doesn't even know about the book of rules that Lola and I have created.

She's talking about the original rules, Rules 1–10. The *Life's Little Rules* page that she cut out of *Ladies' Home Journal,* put in a frame, and hung on our bathroom wall. I guess she thought we would be sitting down an awful lot and could read the rules over and over. And she was right.

Ma is probably referring to Rule #2: *Things always happen for a reason.* But she could also be referring to Rule #6: *Don't expect life to be fair.* I *know* she's not referring to Rule #9: *Treat others the way you want to be treated,* because the folks that want to block our view sure aren't treating us well.

I focus again on what Pop is saying.

"John Shibe and Connie Mack are arguing that there are not enough people filling the stands, and they think we are to blame."

"They don't think we are to blame, dear," Ma interjects.

45

"We're just one part of the problem."

"But nobody who watches the games from here can afford to buy a real ticket!" I exclaim, my voice cracking. "Not this year! What do we have? Ten? Twelve people each game?"

"Twenty today. Back in '29, we squeezed in eighty per roof," Pop chimes in, and Ma gives him a *that's-not-helping* look.

"But they always say things like this. It never happens," Lola says.

"Yes, well this time is more serious," Mr. Sheridan says. "They've already asked the courts to make us take down the bleachers, and the courts sided with us. So now they think the only option is to build a wall to block our view."

Ma picks it up from there. "You remember that when we originally built these stands, we agreed to sell seats only if the ballpark was sold out. That's not happening anymore, and John Shibe has never been happy with this arrangement."

I look down the rows of bleachers on each roof, with the last few happy spectators slowly leaving for their own homes. Mrs. Carson is sitting alone, watching the ballpark empty out. Without people up here watching the games, these rooftop bleachers will be an ugly reminder of something that once was great.

"How can the games sell out if they are trading away all the good players?" Lola interjects.

"I agree," Pop says. "Mack creates a dynasty, and then sells it off. Who wants to see second-rate players lose to the men who used to be our very own all-stars? What a pill." Pop shakes his head.

"The Depression has hurt Shibe Park attendance, just as it's hurt us," Ma says, much calmer. "Every spectator that they see on the rooftop could have been a paying customer inside of Shibe Park. It's created some bad feelings."

Mr. Sheridan chimes back in. "In April, they caught Mr. O'Connor convincing people in the ticket line to come to his roof instead. That made them angry, taking good money-paying folks right out from under their noses. What a fool." He shakes his head. "And last night, Mr. Donahue told us they got a new hot-shot lawyer on their side, Richardson Dilworth." He looks at me. "They still promise you batboy next season?"

"Yes," I reply, straightening up a bit.

"Good." Mr. Sheridan kneels by my seat. "Now don't go and do anything to mess that up. That may be the only way you actually get to see them play."

7

"Why don't you run down to the fair and take your mind off of this," Ma says, searching her housecoat for some change. She hands me two quarters. Lola and I glance at each other, knowing two quarters is too much to spare.

"Very well then," she sighs, taking one quarter back, "but make sure you spend it. This fair is to benefit St. Columba after all."

Neither of us wants to go to the fair yet. We leave by the back ladder and wander aimlessly up and down the streets. There is more activity than normal for a Sunday night, with folks coming and going to the fair. Kids whiz past us on bicycles, holding remnants of cotton candy. Parents sit outside on their porches or stoops, chatting with neighbors.

Will anything ever be the same? I picture a wall big

enough to block us, like some sort of prison. How often do I sit in my bedroom window and gaze out at the ballpark? For hours I watch it—no matter if it's filled with people on a sunny afternoon or completely empty at dusk.

At every turn, something reminds me of the A's. We pass Nick's Restaurant, where the Clubhouse Boys pick up dinners for the team, and Ruvane's barbershop, where players come and go for a shave and a haircut. We make our way to 22nd Street, stop in front of Pop's hardware store and Sheridan's tailoring, scanning down all of the storefronts filled with A's pennant banners under every window. Lola is skipping over cracks, jumping off curbs, and glancing over at me every few seconds. I know she wants to talk about it, but I just want silence.

"Stop!" I say, irritated.

"What?"

"That pebble. You've been kicking it for the whole block. It's getting on my nerves."

"Well your silence is getting on my nerves." She kicks it out to the street and sits on a stoop. "We should head to the fair soon. Besides, you need a new fish. Hey, we should add *that* to the rule book. *Win lucky fish at every school fair.* That should be a new rule. Rule 13a."

"What kind of luck did burying him bring? You heard them. We're losing our view."

"Did you forget that a little someone named *Jimmie Foxx* won that game? On a home run!"

"So?"

"So, we buried that fish to help win games. Not to stop walls."

"I guess. I just really don't want to have to see anyone right now," I confess. She rolls her eyes and pulls my arm.

"Come on. No sense in wallowing."

"Wait," I whisper, but she has already frozen. We both hear the distinct voices of the four Polinski brothers just around the corner.

"We gotta try Lee's Bakery."

"That baker's not gonna have any money."

"Sure will. I heard she stashes her dough right under the floorboard."

"I'll believe it when I see it."

"Just what I heard. And the cellar door only has a padlock."

"Ya think Pa scrounged up some cash today?"

"Nah. He's only good for playin' the street number and gamblin' it away."

They turn the corner and stop in their tracks at the sight of us.

"Heya, guys." Boy, do I sound stupid.

"You spyin' on us again, Jimmy Frank?" the oldest one says. They gather around, standing tall with arms crossed.

"What? No. We were just sitting here. About to head to the fair."

"I hope you didn't hear nothin'. For your sake."

"Didn't hear anything. Honest."

"We were just sitting here. *You* were walking," Lola says, and I shove her with my elbow.

"We gotta go." We squeeze through them, walking briskly in the direction of Reyburn Park.

"Hey, Frank," I hear one of them say, but I keep looking forward.

"That was close," I finally exhale.

"We need to warn Michele," Lola says.

"Who?"

"The baker. Ma knows her."

"I doubt it will matter. You should hear them at school. Every day they're talkin' about breaking into one place or another. They've probably moved onto another scheme by now."

"Why don't you ever tell anyone?"

"No way. They'll kill me if I snitch. You know that."

"How would they know it was you? They think the *baker* has some hidden money just because they heard she has *dough*," she cackles.

"They really are dim," I agree.

"Okay, enough about the Polinskis. We have a plan of our own, so let's move."

"What?"

"It's time to win you a new pet fish."

We make our way to Reyburn Park and the annual

St. Columba fair. Just around the corner on Lehigh Avenue, Reyburn is a perfect little patch of green in the middle of the city, named after an old mayor who threw out the first pitch in Shibe Park back in '09.

"Where are the rides?" Lola asks. We scan the park. There are no rides, or big prize tables, or anything that resembles school fairs from the past. The big fancy signs have been replaced with handwritten posters, and the familiar sound of ringing bells is missing.

"Too expensive, I guess."

"They sure are trying to make it look like a real fair. Get a load of that," she points to the fairground ahead. Before us are handmade games trying very much to look like the real thing, now staffed by nuns, instead of game vendors, dressed in flat caps and money aprons.

There are darts, a Popeye Pipe Toss, and something called The Sword Swallower. Beyond it, I see a BB gun shooting gallery with playing cards propped up as targets. Santa, Ralph, and Matty are all taking turns with the mallet to try and ring the top bell. With every unsuccessful bang of strength, nearby girls giggle louder.

Beyond them is the ring-a-bottle toss. "Come on," I say, pulling her. "They have goldfish prizes. It's five cents a toss. That's five tries."

"Duh," she laughs. "Let me go first."

"No way! Like you said, it's my pet fish. *I* have to win for it to be lucky. And if I win on the first try, we can still buy some funnel cake and give a dime back to Ma."

"First try!" Lola laughs again. "I won't hold my breath."

"Lola, if I land it on the first try, this fish will bring us luck and that wall will not go up."

"Well, here's hoping." She stands aside. Santa, Ralph, and Matty show up, and all eyes are on me.

I give the money to Sister Lucille, the nun running the game and a teacher at St. Mary's. She hands me the ring and I concentrate.

"So serious, this one," Sister Lucille says to Lola.

The noise around me is muffled except for Lola's *"Come on, Jimmy. Light toss, Jimmy."* I fix my gaze on a milk bottle near the middle, flick my wrist, and toss the ring.

I hold my breath as it bounces off one bottle and skims the others, only to land on the very last corner bottle. It shifts, and just like that, settles around the bottleneck. We all jump up and down and squeal like three-year-olds.

"Winner," Sister Lucille says with dry enthusiasm. "Now pick out a fish."

I hold up my new fish, and we look into the jar from opposite sides. Lola's eyes look especially big through the water, and her hair glows as the sun is beginning to set behind us.

"So, what's his name?" she asks.

"I have to think of a good one." I watch the bright

orange fish slowly swimming in circles without a care in the world. He makes his way to the surface in search of food. I realize that I'm hungry too.

The fair is winding down. Hal, our favorite pretzel vendor from Shibe Park, is closing up and waves us over.

"Here, take the extras home." He hands us a bag of hot, soft pretzels. "No sense in wasting."

"Thanks!" we both say at the same time. I give one each to Ralph, Matty, and Santa on their way out.

"Oh wow," Santa says. "Pa will love it."

"Hey, you want to take the rest home?" I offer, remembering they packed up the store earlier today.

"Maybe one more for Ma?" he says, and his cheeks flush with embarrassment. I hand him half the bag.

"Thanks, Jimmy." He gives me a final wave and follows Matty and Ralph toward home.

With everything closed, we make our way to the far end of the park, away from the fair.

For a brief time, we had forgotten all about the wall.

We settle at the Reyburn roundabout, a metal disk that spins like a small merry-go-round. Lola sits on the edge, leaning her shoulder and head on one of the handles. She dangles her legs to the ground, slowly moving it in circles with her feet.

"Bing Miller," I say to Lola, still looking at my new good-luck charm through his small glass jar. "I'm going to name him Bing Miller. If he's going to bring luck with this right-field wall, then I'm going to name him after our right fielder."

"Sounds good," Lola says with her eyes closed, soaking in the setting sun.

I put Bing Miller in the shade of a tree, sit down, and lay back in the tall, thick grass.

No worries. Just peace and quiet.

"It sure does sound final," Lola finally says, breaking the silence. So much for *no worries.* "I can't believe it. I just can't believe it."

I choose not to respond and just let her keep chattering away. She's been itching to talk about the wall since we left the rooftop. Her voice becomes softer and louder as she moves the roundabout in circles.

A cloud rolls in, and I wait patiently for the sun to come back out. I barely hear Lola mumbling something on the far end of her circular trip. Her voice is strained, and the words become clear.

"I said: CUT IT OUT!"

My eyes pop open. It's not clouds blocking the sun, but one of the Polinski brothers, whose dirty smile stretches across his face. He rests his right foot on my chest as I try to rise up.

"Don't even think about it, Jimmy Frank," he grunts.

Again, I hear Lola cry out. I crane my neck up to see her clinging to the metal handle of the roundabout. Two other Polinskis have taken hold of the ride and are running it in circles, picking up speed. Lola is yelling for them to stop, but they just keep laughing and egging each other on.

I don't have a good view, but it looks like the youngest Polinski brother walks over and tries to stop it, without success. She passes in flashes, going by too fast for me to help. If her hand slips, she will fly off and crash on the hard ground. Again I try to sit up, but the Polinski steps harder on my chest.

"Aw, Jimmy Frank. Is that your girlfriend?" he taunts.

"Hey Polinskis!" I yell at them. "Quit picking on a girl!"

They immediately let go. The roundabout continues to circle, with its momentum doing the work now. The three other Polinski brothers come toward me like they've been looking for a fight all day. The oldest brother crouches down to my level.

"What was that?" he says, close to my face.

"Come on, guys. I said leave her alone. She didn't do anything to you." My voice cracks.

"You can't talk to us like that. You hear me?"

"Yeah, sure guys," I say, trying again to shift out from under the boot.

"I don't think you did," one of them says while they grab my wrists and ankle. "And you know what we can do to you."

Only my left leg is free, until the oldest Polinski points

to his youngest brother and motions for him to grab my foot.

"Let's just leave them be," the youngest brother replies.

"*Get it now!*" he says with such force that the Polinski jumps to attention and picks up my foot. We make eye contact before he quickly looks away. Pinned down and completely helpless, I hold my breath and stare up at the clouds, waiting for the first strike.

"I know, guys. Come on, we didn't do anything to you," I plead.

"You were spyin' on us earlier. Now how can we be sure you won't snitch?"

"Snitch on what?" I say in a panic.

"Let's scram before they catch us," the oldest one says. I strain to lift my head and see Sister Lucille and another nun walking near us, heading toward the exit.

The other brothers let go of my arms and legs and follow, except the one with his foot on my chest.

"I said come on," the oldest one snips. He picks up our bag of hot soft pretzels and takes them with him.

The Polinski brother takes his foot off and I exhale. I try to catch my breath, turn on my side, and start to cough uncontrollably. I look up toward the roundabout when I feel a stabbing pain to my head. I grunt as my eyes blur with tears and my head slumps back to the ground.

"Keep your mouth shut or you'll have more than just

a boot to the face," he says as he walks away to catch up with his brothers.

I try to focus my eyes on Lola, who is now in the grass and doubled over, clutching her stomach.

"Jimmy?" I hear her say as my head rests back on the ground. She crawls over to me and collapses. Lying under the tree, we take deep breaths.

"One day, we'll figure out the right way to handle them," she says, finally breaking the silence.

"Lola, there is no right way to handle them."

"We'll see about that." She pulls me up and reaches for my eye. "Ouch."

"Is it that bad?" I touch my eye and wince.

"You could say, 'you should see the other guy.'" She forces an uneasy laugh.

"I can't. They'll know the other guys were the Polinskis."

"Right. It's always the Polinskis."

8

Crowd of 33,318 jams Shibe Park.
—The Sporting News, September 6, 1934

A week later and my bruised eye has changed from black to a greenish yellow. I lie in my bed, trying to read a copy of *Boys' Life*. The team has been on the road, and except for school, it's been easy to avoid everyone.

I tidy my room just to keep busy. I make my bed, lay the afghan across the top, and tuck in the sides. I grab the fish food and peer into the bowl.

"Here you go, Bing." He swims to the top and pokes at his dinner. "What are we gonna do?" I ask the goldfish.

"Jimmy," Ma yells from downstairs. "Dinner's almost ready. Mrs. Carson is joining us."

"Aw, Ma. Do I have to eat with everyone?" I ask, knowing the answer already. "Can Lola come for dinner?"

"Can I bring my friends, too?" Pop yells from the kitchen.

"Very funny." Ma giggles and then calls back up.

59

"It's Sunday—just make sure her parents haven't planned something. And as long as she's ready in ten minutes."

I rush to the window and ring the Bingle, put on my lucky A's cap, and run up the skylight.

"What's going on?" Lola says a minute later.

"Come over for dinner. It's just me with Nina and Mrs. Carson. It'll be awful without you there."

"Why is that so bad?" she says.

"Mrs. Carson is fine, but Nina's been miserable lately. *I'll* be miserable without you."

"I don't know. *Buck Rogers* is coming on the radio soon." She scrunches her face like it's a hard choice, but I know she just wants me to beg.

"Look at my eye!" I rip off my cap. "Don't you feel sorry for me?" I can't help my grin.

"That is so pathetic," she says laughing. "Okay, let me check."

Ten minutes later, we are seated in the living room. Pop is pouring Mrs. Carson some whisky, Ma and Nina are in the kitchen, and Lola and I squish together on the sofa. Benny Goodman's "Moonglow" drifts through the house from the radio.

"Healing well I see?" Mrs. Carson says to me. I can't tell if it's a statement or a question, and I smile awkwardly.

"Yes, ma'am."

"The Polinskis?" she presses.

"Yes, ma'am."

"Want me to change the subject?"

"Yes, ma'am."

Lola blurts out a laugh like she's been holding it in for hours.

"Very well," Mrs. Carson grins. "How's school, Lola?"

"Fine, thank you," Lola says, sitting up straighter.

"And what are you learning right now?"

"Nothing good. It's all girl stuff."

"And that's a problem?" Mrs. Carson laughs.

"Yes. We learn how to type. We have cooking and sewing classes. And all the girls talk about is boys and hairstyles and boys and clothes. And *boys*."

Mrs. Carson laughs again and shakes her head.

"What do you want them to talk about?" Pop asks.

"Anything else!" Lola says, and the words begin to tumble out of her mouth. "Why can't *girl stuff* be science? What about Marie Curie? Or the Equal Rights Amendment? Or at least going to college before getting married!"

"College would suit you well," Mrs. Carson says, and Lola's face brightens with one of the biggest grins I have ever seen.

Ma rings the dinner bell, interrupting our conversation. Nina puts the finishing touches on the place settings in the dining room, and we all take our seats. Pop sits at the head of the table, and Mrs. Carson takes the other end.

"The table looks beautiful," Mrs. Carson says with a genuine smile. In front of us are our formal china plates

61

and crystal glasses. Most of them are now chipped and mismatched. In the middle is a large covered soup tureen.

Pop leads us in a prayer and ends with: "We love our bread, we love our butter, but most of all we love each other." Ma smiles as we all say Amen.

Ma opens the lid and starts to dish out piles of cubed potatoes and sliced hot dogs. Lola and I grin from ear to ear as a mound of Poor Man's Meal sits before us.

"It's not much," Ma says, shaking her head.

"It's GREAT," I say, my mouth full of savory hot dogs fried in butter and onions. Lola smiles in agreement.

"Say, did anyone see the evening *Bulletin*?" Mrs. Carson asks.

"Not yet, ma'am," Lola replies. "Anything good?"

"Some updates on that right-field wall."

"What do they say?" I ask urgently. Lola's eyes catch mine and grow wide.

"I read it. No real change for us," Pop says. "We'll let you know when there's something important to share."

"That wall is ruining everything," Nina says, pushing her food around.

"What do you care? You don't even *like* baseball," I say.

"You don't know anything," she mumbles under her breath and turns to Mrs. Carson. "So, what will happen to you when the wall is built?"

"*Nina*," Ma urges.

"It's fine. It's fine." Mrs. Carson shrugs. "Oh, dear.

What will I do? Try to find another way to make some extra money. Maybe I'll mend socks or make fudge or rent out a room. I can host a coffee klatch. Five cents a person." Mrs. Carson looks to me. "We'll have to be creative, I suppose."

"What's a coffee klatch?" Lola asks.

"Just a gathering," Ma says. "A way for folks to socialize."

"Maybe we can do that, too?" Nina perks up a bit. "What do you think? We can have one every Sunday after church."

"We can talk about it later, honey." Pop pats her hand.

"Why later?" Nina cries. Her sudden change in mood startles us all. "May I please be excused?"

"Yes, dear," Ma says. "We'll clean up." Nina runs from the table, and Lola and I exchange looks.

"What was *that* all about?" I ask.

"She's upset. We've asked her to help us out more," Pop says.

"More hours at the store?"

"No. To find a real job. We told her last Sunday morning," he adds.

"We're depending on her more than we should depend on a fifteen-year-old," Ma sighs. "But we don't want you to worry about it. You're too young to work, or we would have asked you, too."

"I'm *not* too young to work," I urge.

"Not yet," Ma says and pats me on the back. "Nina's

63

old enough to start a real job and bring home a real paycheck."

"Does she need to quit high school?" Lola asks.

"We aren't quite there," Ma says, "but she had her own ideas for the future and she is having trouble adjusting to this reality."

"Like college?" Lola asks.

"Everyone is adjusting," Mrs. Carson says. "It'll affect all of us a little differently. And not just all of us," she waves her hand around the table. "Think of all those home run hitters, too," she says with a smirk and continues eating.

I lower my head and stare at the empty plate. Lola and I don't say a word for the rest of the meal. The adults keep talking about the neighborhood, the news, the church. Mrs. Carson loves the gossip, and Pop is indulging her.

"Can I go out?" Nina says, appearing from the doorway in her coat. "Kate heard there are some jobs at The Hop Inn and we're going to stop by. They close at eight."

"Certainly," Ma says and turns to me. "Would you both like to scoot out, too?"

"Yes, ma'am," we say in unison.

"Can I take the paper?" I add.

"Of course." She sees our clean plates and a look of satisfaction comes across her face. We leave as Ma and Mrs. Carson retire to the living room while Pop fixes them an after-dinner drink.

"Let's go into Shibe," Lola whispers, and I nod. She

64

stuffs the paper in my army bag. We patiently wait for the street to clear and climb the wall. Easy as pie. We settle in the dugout, sitting on the bench and looking drearily at our rooftops in the distance.

Lola quickly reads the article, updating me as she goes along.

"They grouped our families together and tried to sue everyone on the street," she says.

"Everyone? Why would they do that? What else?" I say impatiently.

"Looks like the fire marshal was involved. Now our parents are suing back to stop the wall from being built. But it doesn't look good."

"I guess anyone can build anything they want on their own property. We can build bleachers. They can build a wall."

"Exactly," she says. "And the Spite Fence will be built by the start of the next season."

"Spite Fence?" I look up sharply.

"That's what they are calling it," she says. "The Spite Fence." I stare at right field and feel a strange charge. The Spite Fence. The name burns in me.

"They can't do this," I say in frustration. "Shibe Park had such a big crowd last week."

"That's only because that Detroit pitcher was going for his 17th straight win."

"Did I show you this?" I pull out today's copy of *The Sporting News* and read, "*The Shibe Park management expected a good turn-out, but nothing like the mob that stormed the park. World Series scenes were revived on Lehigh Avenue . . ."*

"I read that, too. Don't just read the parts you want to hear." Lola takes the newspaper from me. She scans the print. *"Attendance on most days at Shibe Park this year has been small, and the record crowd is all the more remarkable as a consequence."*

"I wonder how many home runs Jimmie Foxx has hit to right field."

"Who knows?"

"A lot I bet."

"Why does that matter?"

"Didn't you hear Mrs. Carson tonight? She said, *'think of all those home run hitters.'"* I spring up. "Lola, they really can't do this while Foxx is still on the team!"

"Sure, they can. They can do anything they want."

"Not if someone . . . not if *we* can convince them of *why* it's such a bad idea!"

"Aw, come on, all of our parents can't do anything but *we* are going to do something? Is that right?" Lola says. She climbs the three dugout steps and motions for me to follow.

"Hey, when were you ever one to back away from a challenge?"

"What challenge? And be serious, Jimmy. Your crazy schemes and daydreamer ideas are not going to stop it. Read the article again."

I ignore her and continue. "But without that home run, they would have lost! And don't forget my lucky fish. That was *your* idea!"

"Yes, Jimmy. Without that home run, they would have lost. And now you have a lucky fish. And without some sleep, I'm never going make it through Sister Lucille's handwriting lesson. And if we are caught doing anything crazy, you're out as batboy."

We leave through the back door and continue our normal walk home, but I can't let it go. I pull Lola into the shadows of the grandstand entrance and hold both her shoulders.

"I have an idea. A really good idea." I'm grinning from ear to ear. "Just hear me out."

"Okay, okay. Settle down!" she says.

"You mark my words, Lola. I am going to save our view."

9

To think of a team equipped with such a brilliant infield and a mighty outfield as the Athletics, finishing in seventh place, suggests a problem very difficult to fathom.
—The Sporting News, September 20, 1934

It's been three weeks since we found out about the Spite Fence, two weeks since I came up with a plan to save the view, and one week since Lola and I figured out exactly how to make it happen. Today is the day.

I pace on Lola's porch, waiting for her to walk to school. Where is she? I lean against the rail, picking at the peeling paint. I rang that bell five minutes ago. She should be out here by now.

"Jimmy Frank!" Lola's mother bursts out the door in her housecoat and slippers. I jump off the ledge and stand straight up.

"Good morning, Mrs. Sheridan." I clear my throat. I'm not used to her tone and answer more formally than usual. She looks from me, to the peeled paint, then back to me.

"Are you planning on painting our porch, dear?"

"No, ma'am."

"Well, then, I would appreciate it if you didn't ruin what paint is left," she sighs.

"Yes, ma'am. I'm sorry."

Lola finally makes her way outside and saves me. She looks at the two of us, grabs me by my bag, and pulls me down the steps.

"See ya, Ma," she calls. I wave and turn away.

"I think I just ruined your Mom's morning," I say.

"Nah," Lola says. "She's always like that now." We wave to Mrs. Carson like we do every morning. She waves back from her porch.

"Ma's like that now, too," I confess a few steps later. "She just keeps saying that she's 'waiting for the day' for the team to take their hardware business elsewhere. But I don't know. I just can't see that happening."

"What do you mean you *just can't see that happening*? It's not just a wall, Jimmy. You have to know that." We are crossing 23rd Street now, and some other kids are making their way out of their homes. She ignores them and continues.

"Think about it. They sued us to take down the stands, and they lost. Now we are suing them to stop the wall from being built. Whether we win or lose, there are going to be bad feelings."

"You sound like an adult."

"Just repeating what the adults are saying," she replies.

"So, does your Mom think they'll give the uniforms to someone else, just because you live on 20th Street?"

"Who knows. But she's nervous," she says. "And you should be nervous too."

"What? Why?"

"I wonder if they'll still give batboy to someone who has bleachers on their roof." Lola eyes me, looking for a reaction. I keep looking forward.

"I guess we'll see," I say firmly. I am not going to let them take this away too. I change the subject. "After the doubleheader today, we'll be on the right track." She just looks at me and smiles. I'm not sure she actually believes our plan is going to work.

"So, let's go over it again," she says, trying to sound positive. "I'll pretend to be Jimmie Foxx."

"Okay," I reply.

"*Son, my home runs usually go to left field,*" Lola says in a deep voice.

"Not the last one," I mumble, and Lola stops in her tracks.

"That's not good enough. Try again. You have to be able to convince the great Jimmie Foxx, an MVP, of why he has to go up against Shibe and Mack."

"You're right." I straighten up and clear my throat. "Mr. Foxx, two years ago you missed the home run record by only three runs. There are always a few that go to right field. And if you want to chase that record, building a wall will almost guarantee you never reach it."

"That's better," she says. "Listen, you don't know how much time you'll have before they kick you out. I can't be there with you, so every word you say has to mean something."

Lola always knows how to put things into perspective.

"I wish you could go in with me," I say.

"Jimmy, we both know a girl in the clubhouse will draw too much attention. Besides, they're not ready for me yet."

"Probably not."

"Now, I'll help you sneak inside Shibe Park. Just remember everything we talked about. It's a double-header, so try to speak to him before game one starts. Be strong. Don't stumble over your words. And remember Rule #4: *Look people in the eye*." Lola smiles nervously as she says this, noticing Santa, Ralph, Matty, and a few other boys waiting for me on the next block. The Polinski brothers are also approaching the group from the other direction.

"I gotta go," I say quickly.

"How can you still walk to school with them?" she points to my eye.

"It'll be worse if I don't." My face becomes hot. "There is no way to avoid them. I just have to act like everything is normal."

"I will never, ever, understand boys," she exclaims,

and turns right to head to her school. "I'll see you in six hours." Her voice trails off as she walks away.

My stomach swirls with nerves. If I can make it through today, sneak into the ballpark, and find Jimmie Foxx, everything will be okay. But first, I just have to get through the Polinskis. Unharmed.

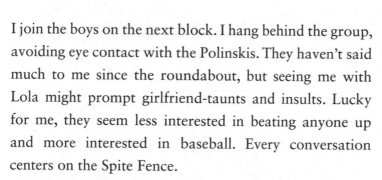

10

I join the boys on the next block. I hang behind the group, avoiding eye contact with the Polinskis. They haven't said much to me since the roundabout, but seeing me with Lola might prompt girlfriend-taunts and insults. Lucky for me, they seem less interested in beating anyone up and more interested in baseball. Every conversation centers on the Spite Fence.

"My dad has a friend, who has a friend who works at the courthouse, who says the judge is probably going to side with the A's," Matty says.

"My old man says you can build whatever you want on your own *damn property*," the oldest Polinski grunts in his father's gruff voice. "I hope they build that wall." He spits to the side, hitting Santa's shoe. Ralph catches Santa's eye and shakes his head, as if to say *keep quiet*.

We turn toward St. Columba, the Irish church and

boys' school. I continue to lag behind the group. As they walk ahead, I wonder what would happen if I actually did what Lola always says I should. I close my eyes, picturing the moment.

"Hey Polinski," I'd shout. "We aren't your punching bags. Keep your hands to yourself from now on!" All the neighborhood kids would be impressed as the brothers run down the block. Ralph, Matty, and Santa would pat me on the back with *you did it!* and *good job!* coming from all directions. Lola would be on a nearby stoop, watching with a big grin.

I come back to reality when I stumble on the cobblestone, barely catching myself before falling. Everyone turns and laughs. I laugh nervously and continue to walk.

Finally, at school, I can relax. With adults around, the Polinskis will keep away, at least a little. We all stand in front of the brick church. The large, round, stained-glass window is glistening in the morning sun, shooting colorful diamonds on the steps as we walk into school. I look up at its image of Jesus with outstretched arms, a yellow glow encircling him. The rumor is that if you catch him looking you straight in the eye, it will bring good luck. I stretch my neck to catch his gaze, but no luck today.

Father Ryan greets us as we enter, shooing us into the class and closing the doors tight. He runs the place with his own set of rules, and being on time is a big one. We sit alphabetically, with hats off, good posture, and no talking. There is only one large classroom for the school, which means the four Polinski brothers are a couple rows behind me.

"Take out your pencils," he says, handing out our black and white writing journals. "We are going to do a little exercise. Who can tell me what it means to be spiteful?"

The room buzzes at the word "spite."

"You all know I'm a baseball fan," he lectures, waving his arms to highlight the A's pennants all over the room. "And with all this talk about the Spite Fence, I think a lesson in spite is appropriate. Now, Mr. Frances, can you tell me what it means to be spiteful?"

I squirm in my seat and straighten my back. "Yes, Father. You are spiteful when you do something just to, ah, spite someone else."

Someone snickers behind me.

"Yes, son." Father is now standing beside my desk, looking forward. "And what does that mean? To, as you say, *spite someone else.*"

"Well. To do it just to be mean. To do it because you want to get back at someone."

"Very good." He starts walking up and down the aisle. "Mr. Frances, have you ever done something out of spite?"

He cannot be serious.

"Yes, sir." My face is hot. I'm not *in* confession. I start searching in my head for something that I did to Nina.

Something not too embarrassing. Like the time I threw her stuffed Teddy Roosevelt bear out the window into the street below. I squirm in my seat.

"I would imagine we all have done something spiteful in our lives." He lets me off the hook. I exhale and look at Matty, who puts his hand over his mouth to stop from laughing. I look down as I hold in my own laugh, too.

"I probably did a few things myself as a boy," he continues. "Even in the *Bible*, there are stories about spite. And it goes on today. There are several reasons why someone might become spiteful." Father makes his way to the chalkboard. "Can anyone tell me some of these reasons?"

Some kids around me are raising their hands. They say things like "hurt feelings." Someone behind me mentions an unfair game of half-ball, and others talk about parents losing jobs or having to shut down a family business.

I raise my hand and wait for him to call on me.

"Greed," I say.

"Yes, Mr. Frances. Greed. Well done." He writes the word up on the blackboard and stands in front of all of us. "And let me tell you why building that wall at Shibe Park is full of greed and spite."

11

School ends, finally. I walk slowly and stop to tie my shoe, letting everyone else go ahead of me.

I try to walk casually toward Shibe and the double-header, but the excitement quickens my steps and I have to consciously slow myself down. I say hello to some of the grandparents sitting on their porches on 23rd Street, and turn at Santa's old corner store, now boarded up. A block later, I finally give in and run the rest of the way to Shibe Park, hopping over curbs and faintly hearing a *where you goin' in such a rush?* from someone to my left.

I arrive just in time to see the groups of kids walk up. Lola is heading toward me, and Operation Knothole Gang is ready to go. We both study the crowd.

"Just like any other Knothole Gang day," she says. "We'll blend right in. Time for Rule #15: *Watch games from inside the ballpark on Knothole Gang days.*"

"Yep. They're wearing red today." I rummage through my bag, searching through the colored badges left on the ground after games. Over the years we've collected them all—blue, yellow, green. I pull out two red badges looking good as new.

"Where are they from today?" she wonders aloud.

"I don't know. Maybe West Philly? Or the suburbs? Sure is a big crowd."

"I wonder who paid for all their tickets. That's got to be an awful lot of money."

"And our ticket," I grin, handing her the badge and chain. She slides it over her head.

"Well whoever it is, I bet they'd help us stop that wall from being built. We'll all have to watch games through the knotholes in the fence if it goes up."

"That's not going to happen. Not after our plan works," I say and motion for us to join the crowd.

We lag a little behind the group as they head inside, and I scan the turnstile for a ticket-taker who doesn't already know me. Normally, this is all a breeze, but today there is more at stake. My heart thumps a few times, and I stop for a minute to catch my breath.

"Over here," Lola says, looking back and resting her hand on my arm. "It's easy-peasy. We've done this before." I nod.

We choose the ticket-taker on the right, and slide in line behind two ladies chatting over what concession

78

food to eat first. They decide on Wilbur's Famous Chocolate. That sounds pretty good to me.

The first lady quickly enters the ballpark, but the second one is having trouble with the turnstile, an old, rusty piece of junk with black paint chipping off the top. It jams and traps her as she tries to push it forward.

"Hold on, Miss. I'll help." I take the metal section behind her and place my hands on top of the bar, ready to push. The ticket-taker slips his hand into the section in front of her, ready to pull.

"One, two, three," I say. Together we push–pull. The turnstile jerks, lurching the lady forward and into the ballpark corridor. I follow with a stumble, and I hear her cry out in pain. A small blood trail reveals a tiny cut on her leg, thanks to what looks like a broken, rusty pedal at the turnstile base.

"That doesn't look too good, Miss," I say. "We can show you to the first aid station."

Lola comes through the turnstile next, and we brush the rust and dirt off our clothes. The line begins to back up, and the ticket-taker gives us a grateful nod and points in the direction of the first aid station. I assure him that I know the way, and together we disappear into the Shibe Park crowd.

"That was easy," I whisper. Lola nods in agreement.

Lola and I take the two women to the first aid station and say goodbye, walking swiftly to where Ronny the

Clubhouse Boy usually hangs out before games. It's about ten minutes before we spot him near the door, where all the players are getting ready.

"Hey Ronny, over here." Ronny looks up and smiles. He is much taller than me, skinny, and almost frail-looking in the A's uniform. He makes his way over. Lola turns to a concession sign and pretends to study the menu.

"Jimmy Frank, what brings you inside?"

"I need to see Jimmie Foxx. I have to ask him a question. Can I bring his meal today?"

"Too late." Ronny holds out a dirty plate and a greasy brown bag that has all the earmarks of Nick's Restaurant from around the corner. My shoulders sink. "Besides, his tip is too big for me to pass it up. What's so urgent?"

"Just a question. Any other time I can catch him?"

"He asked me to bring him peach pie between games," he says pulling out a one-dollar bill.

"Wow, he's a big tipper!"

"Yep. But it's for the whole doubleheader," he says, examining the bill.

"So if you already have the money, what does it matter?"

This is not ideal. The clubhouse between a double-header is always more hectic than beforehand. But at least I'll have a reason to be in there.

"Alright." He's eyeing me up. "But if you get yourself caught, you didn't see me today—you did this all on your own."

I agree, and we shake on it. I spot Lola and shrug my shoulders. No sense in being upset. We have a plan. Now there is nothing we can do but find a seat, enjoy the first game, and practice how I am going to approach a two-time MVP.

The game is fast, and it feels a little like the guys on the field want to finish this one quickly. I bet the players hate doubleheaders during the last week of a losing season, when both teams are out of contention for the pennant.

For most of the game, we sit in some open seats along the first-base side. I keep my eye on Jimmie Foxx for any sign—something I can use to convince him to help me. I'm not sure what I'm looking for, but I still keep a close watch. He's a keen player, gazing toward the hitter, motioning to the rest of the infield, using his signs. No matter what place the team is in, Jimmie is out to win. That's what makes him an MVP.

It's the top of the eighth inning when I notice two security guards hanging around us.

"Lola." I nod my head in their direction.

"Wanna go for a pop?" Lola says loud enough for them to hear and tugs my shirt sleeve. "Come on."

The first guard isn't paying attention anymore, but the second one makes eye contact with me when I stand up. I quickly look down and pretend to check my pocket for change.

"Where's your group?" he says as we pass. We stop and slowly turn around. I open my mouth but can't find

81

any words. Lola takes my hand in hers.

"Just on the other side. We just wanted to sneak away for a little," she says in a sweet, soft voice. She blushes and actually looks lovestruck and embarrassed.

"Okay, run along. No funny business. You aren't supposed to leave the group."

"Yes, sir," we both say and turn away. We lose them in the crowd and find an empty seat just by third base, below the left-field stands.

"How did you do that? Your face was bright red! Just like that!" I snap my fingers.

"Maybe I'll be a big-screen actress, or a Broadway star." She flips her hair and poses.

"You'd be good!"

Lola is still pretending to pose when I glance at the field and see Jimmie Foxx step out of the dugout. As he approaches the plate, I overhear a father telling his son about Foxx's home run in game one of the 1929 World Series against Chicago.

I remember listening to the radio announcer that day, when he coined the now-famous phrase, *Goodbye, Mr. Spalding!* It was the first game of my first A's World Series. I was eight years old.

Every inch of our house was packed with neighbors. Lola, Santa, Ralph, Matty, and I were on the steps overlooking the living room through the spindles, watching Ma and Pop and all their friends gathered around the radio. It was the seventh inning when Jimmie Foxx hit the bomb to tie the game at one apiece. The entire house erupted when we heard the crack of the bat and the announcer yell, "GOODBYE, MR. SPALDING!"

Goodbye, Mr. Spalding! It was like the announcer was shouting to a friend who was unexpectedly leaving the ballpark. With that call, baseballs became more than just a white ball with random words and colored thread. Baseballs suddenly had a personality.

Bing Miller came through in the ninth to drive in two runs for the win. Jimmie and Bing. And Mr. Spalding. It always seems to come down to them. The memory is as clear as if it happened yesterday.

"Snap out of it!" Lola nudges my shoulder, and I come back to focus.

Foxx hasn't been great in the batter's box today. He's been up three times with nothing to show for it. The game is tied 4–4. The players look lazy, and the fans seem bored.

The view from this side of the field is different than I am used to. I hear some betting from the left-field stands. You'd think two guys gambling would be a little quieter. I look up and realize I can see my whole family watching from the roof.

Pop has his friends around him. He stretches his arms out with some sort of punchline and everyone laughs. Ma is leaning on the side of the bleachers, watching the game. Nina is by herself at the top, arms crossed. Santa, Ralph, and Matty are in the usual spot, probably wondering where we are. I wave my arms above my head.

"They can't see you, dummy!" Lola says, and I slowly bring them down.

A chorus of giggles breaks out to the right and I notice three Knothole girls. Two of them start to whisper when I look. The third looks annoyed. She reminds me of Lola.

Something beneath the left-field stands catches my eye.

"What is that thing?" I squint, not sure of what I am seeing. Something sleek and long, deep red with a white pinstripe.

"Is that a *boat*?" Lola exclaims.

We both lean for a better look when we hear the crack. The ball is soaring high above the field. Washington's Fred Sington in right field is stepping back and back and back. *He's going to catch it.*

The ball starts to drop as Fred leaps, using the right-field wall as a boost, and stretching his glove hand toward the top edge. He momentarily grabs the ball, which sticks out of his glove like an ice cream cone—*gasp from the crowd!*—before falling over the fence for a home run. It was the greatest almost-catch I have ever seen.

But he *didn't* catch it.

"GOODBYE, MR. SPALDING!" I shout.

"Now *that's* something you should say to Foxx today!" She shakes her head in disbelief. "What are the chances he hits a right-field home run today! Of all days! Who would have guessed!"

"I think it's our lucky fish," I reply. We both can't stop smiling as he finishes rounding the bases. "That's two, you know."

"What's two?"

"His last two home runs went to right field. That doesn't happen with a Spite Fence."

"This really could work," Lola says.

"It will work. Jimmie Foxx will help us stop this wall."

12

*The Athletics took a double header from
the Washington Senators, 5 to 4 and 3 to 0.
Jimmie Foxx' forty-fourth homer of the season
helped the A's win the opener . . .*
—The Sporting News, September 27, 1934

I stand by the clubhouse door, holding Jimmie Foxx's peach pie and patiently waiting for the players to return. The hallway is jammed with happy fans taking a break between games. They are all telling the same story, reliving that Foxx home run over the right-field wall. The security guards are laughing and patting each other on the back. Nobody is paying attention to me. I take a deep breath and easily slip inside.

"Mr. Foxx?" I say, peering around the corner inside the clubhouse. "I have your pie."

"Over here," he calls, from the back. I make my way through the players, holding a piece of warm peach pie tightly in both hands.

"Where's Ronny?" he asks, surprised.

"He needed to take care of something. He asked me

86

to bring this to you. I'm going to work for the A's next year." I sound ridiculous.

"Yeah, where?" he asks, taking the pie. He doesn't tell me to scram, and I linger a few feet away.

"Batboy. I was told to come by after the season."

"A new batboy, huh? Did ya ask them to heat up my pie?"

"Yes, sir. Is it cold?"

"It's just right," he replies, licking the fork. "And I do love a warm pie."

"Me too. It's one of my rules."

"What rules?"

Why did I say that?

"Well, I have these rules, see. And Rule #18 is never to eat cold pie." I sound like a dummy.

"I like that rule," Jimmie Foxx says. "Sure could use someone like you in the clubhouse."

I don't want clubhouse duty—running errands and cleaning up after the players. Except for the tips, there is nothing good about it. I'd much rather be in the dugout.

"Sure thing, Mr. Foxx." The MVP thanks me and starts looking for some change.

"I don't need a tip. Ronny took care of me." I pause and clear my throat. "Mr. Foxx. Can I ask you a question?"

"Depends on what it is," he replies. I can't tell if he is kidding. He is kind of like a happy-go-lucky gentleman combined with a cowboy from the West.

"Right. Well, Mr. Foxx." I clear my throat again. "I'm wondering what you'll do when they build that wall in right field."

"Aw, they've been rambling on about that for years. Free baseball. Outlaw stands. Stealing the profits. I've heard it since I got here in '27. It'll never happen." He's so casual. He really believes it.

"I'm not so sure, Mr. Foxx. There was some sort of lawsuit, and the folks in the neighborhood say the wall is going up for sure."

"Like I said, I don't think it will go up. Stop worrying," he says. "Besides, most of my dingers go left."

"Not the last two at home. The game winner against Lefty Grove a few weeks ago, and today's. If that wall goes up, they'd be doubles at most."

"True," he replies. "True."

"You know, I live right across the street. It will really change the neighborhood, too."

"Not sure I can do anything about it, kid." He leans back and watches me for a moment.

"Any chance you might put in a good word to Mr. Mack? Remind him that it might take some runs away from you? From the team? Don't forget, in '32, you were only three runs from beating Babe Ruth's home run record."

He looks at me for a few more seconds. It seems like hours.

"What's your name, kid?"

"James Frances, but everyone calls me Jimmy Frank."

"That name's got a nice ring to it," he chuckles. "You sure are persistent, Jimmy Frank." He shakes my hand. "I'll mention it. Doubt it will make a difference, but I'll mention it. I sure will have a lot of time to talk to him. He's got some of us going on a baseball tour after the season. Barnstormin' Canada and then heading to Japan to show us off."

I nod and smile. The Japanese all-star tour is well known among fans, and it's all the papers have been about lately. "Thanks, Mr. Foxx. Wow, thanks. Good luck in game two."

He gives me a two-finger salute, and I know it is time to leave. I float out of the clubhouse, through the hallway, and around the turnstile. I'm ready to burst and can't get out of the ballpark fast enough.

"Woo-hoo!!" I finally yell, once I'm on the street. Nobody even notices, and I begin to sprint home. *It's going to work!* I can't wait to be on the roof. I can't wait to tell everyone.

The street is game-time crowded and I skip in between food carts and jump over curbs. A half-ball barely misses my head, and I dodge out of the way. I hear the Polinskis' laughter and break to my left before they can nail me. Nobody can touch me today.

"Ma, Pop. MA, POP! LOLA!" I yell their names from the street, all the way up the stairs, climbing the ladder, and through the hallway skylight.

"Goodness, Jimmy!" Ma comes to me. "What's wrong?"

I rest my hands on both knees to catch my breath. "Wait 'till you hear this. Hey Lola, Mr. Sheridan! Come here!"

Once everyone is gathered, I tell the story. How the great Jimmie Foxx is going to save the view. How *he* wants to save his home runs. How *he* is going to talk to Connie Mack when they tour Japan, and how *he* is going to shut this stupid idea down.

I finish my story out of breath again. I look around, waiting for the applause and the 'great job!' Only Lola is beaming, writing furiously in her tablet. Pop and Mr. Sheridan exchange glances, and Ma comes over and puts her arm around my shoulder.

"Well done, my dear," she says, in a soft-spoken voice that I hear her use while serving in the church soup line. "Well done."

"Well done? What's wrong with everyone!" I'm frustrated by their ho-hum looks and their stolen glances at each other. It's like someone died, and I am the only one who doesn't know. "Didn't you hear what I said? Jimmie Foxx is going to save our view!"

"Let's hope," Ma offers.

"You've all given up already, haven't you?" I ask. Nobody really answers. They just look at each other, and from the corner of my eye, I see Nina walking toward us. Her eyes are bloodshot.

"You think just because you brought him some warm peach pie, he's going to make it his life's mission to make sure they don't build the wall? A guy like that has more important things to think about than you." Nina storms off in tears before I can respond.

"What was that all about? This will help her, too!" I look at Ma.

"Yes, well, until that happens, she still needs to find a job. Nobody is willing to hire her. Not yet, at least. Unless she quits school, she doesn't have many choices," Ma says.

"You did good today, kid," Pop says. He tussles my hair on his way to the skylight. "I'll go talk with her."

"Yes, you did very well today. We are just so tired of it all. I'm sorry, dear," Ma motions her hand toward Shibe Park where game two is under way.

"Hey, Jimmy. Run down and buy me a Red-Hot and a pop?" Mr. Fletcher asks, and I realize we still have a few weekday customers for game two. He hands me a quarter. "Keep the change."

I tug Lola's sleeve and we start the climb down the ladder leading to the backyard.

I glance back up toward the rooftop, watching as it starts to feel farther and farther away.

13

*There was some doubt up to sailing time
if Jimmie Foxx would make the trip at all.*
—The Sporting News, October 18, 1934

Despite everyone else's lukewarm reaction to my Jimmie
Foxx encounter, for weeks I am still floating on air. I
know they don't think it will work, but I have a feeling
about him.

"Jimmy! Jimmy!" I hear one morning, followed by an
excited knock on the door.

"Hello, dear," Ma welcomes Lola as she rushes past
her to the kitchen.

"Hi, Mrs. Frances! Jimmy, did you see the news?"

"What news?" Jimmy asked.

"Jimmie Foxx is in the hospital!"

"*What?*"

She scans the newspaper in her hands. "It's right here.
Barney Brown, some lefty in Canada, hit him square in
the head. Knocked him out cold!"

"Let me see that!" I grab it from her and look at each

page for more information. "Oh no. He's in the hospital."

"Sorry, kid." Pop slaps my back and starts to clear the breakfast dishes.

"Oh no," I say over and over again. "He just has to be okay."

"You won't hear much news from Canada. Or Japan," Pop says. "The players aren't due back until the end of December."

"I'm sure he's okay, sweetheart," Ma says. "Now let's not become too distracted. Don't forget it's inventory day."

"What?" I look up. "Oh, right. Lola, come with me. Let's check the other papers first."

She nods, and we rush out the door, practically knocking the milkman down along the way.

"Foxx never gets hit by pitches," I pout. None of the other papers had anything to add. "Now he has more important things on his mind."

"If he got hit as hard as they say, he might not have anything on his mind," Lola says.

"Right. Maybe he's asking the nurse to warm up his peach pie," I say sarcastically. "What a stupid idea anyway. I bet he forgot about me as soon as I walked out of the clubhouse."

"Well, we can't control anything about it," she says.

"That's the problem. We can't control anything about it."

"We *can* control finishing this inventory so we can get to the park faster."

"You're right. Let's hurry."

An hour later, we are deep into the inventory, counting boxes of nails and hammers and hoses and bolts.

"Two Disston D-12 hand saws," I yell down to Lola from high on the ladder.

"24- or 26-inch?" she yells back up, checking the clipboard.

"Um, 26. One Philadelphia Tool Company broad axe," I yell back down.

"Did you say one, Jimmy?" Pop calls, turning down the radio. Bing Crosby is crooning "Just One More Chance."

"Yes, Pop. And one Peck, Stow & Wilcox 6-inch monkey wrench, Cleveland," I reply. Pop is at the front with Mr. Fletcher, and I hear him say that he'll run down to Fishtown to pick up a few broad axes, but he'll let the Peck wrenches sell out.

"Desperate times, Fletch," Pop says. "We can't be shipping in things from Ohio anymore."

A few more guys come in to talk while Lola and I continue the work. One of them mentions the other big headline in today's paper.

"Babe Ruth? Manage the A's?"

"It'll never happen," Pop says. "Mack will never leave. And Babe will never come, no matter what the headline says."

"Babe Ruth," I whisper to Lola. "I could meet him next year, you know."

"You are going to meet a lot of great players," she whispers back.

"Except Jimmie Foxx, if his head isn't fixed."

"Well you already met him, anyway," she says. "You know he might have already said something to Connie Mack. Before he got beaned in the head."

"You think?"

"Why not? They've been traveling a lot already."

"I sure hope so. All the players will thank me next year when they learn that I stopped the wall from being built." I grin at the thought.

"The pitchers won't thank you."

"Good point," I laugh.

"Hey Jimmy, what's so funny up on that top shelf?" Mr. Fletcher says.

I clear my throat, "Nothing, Mr. Fletcher." Quickly, I get back to work. I much prefer it when they don't even realize we're here. I hear one of them call me a "wide-eyed daydreamer" from below. Two aisles later and the men are still in the store.

"Sure would go faster if they did some work!" Lola says in a huff.

With each beer, their conversation becomes louder. In between inventory numbers, I hear bits and pieces:

. . . seven daughters!

. . . lost two big orders this week alone . . .

. . . Eagles will never be as good as the Frankford Yellow Jackets . . .

. . . arrested some guy named Hauptmann. Bruno Hauptmann . . .

. . . Bing Miller released . . .

I jerk and the ladder shakes a bit under me. Lola grabs and steadies it. We look at each other, eyes wide and straining to hear. I whisper *no, no, no,* and Lola covers her mouth in disbelief. Not Bing Miller. Not our right fielder. Not my lucky fish.

"I don't believe it." Pop sounds just as shocked as us.

"It's in last night's *Evening Bulletin*. Released and taking a manager role with some minor league team in Richmond."

"Virginia?"

"Yeah, Virginia," Mr. Fletcher says. There is a swoosh that sounds a lot like a newspaper hitting the back of someone's head.

"He's better off. With that Spite Fence coming," Pop says.

"Say, when's that hearing?"

"The end of November. That'll settle it all, Fletch. No more appeals, no more fights. By noon on the thirtieth, we'll know if the wall will be built or not." There is a long pause. "That lawyer Dilworth is one slick character."

"Tryin' to make a name for himself," Mr. Fletcher says in agreement. "So, we'll know on the thirtieth. The day after Thanksgiving, no less."

"Hey, let's invite Dilworth to Kilroy's Tap Room and

pour some liquor in him for the holiday. Throw him off his game the next day," Pop jabs.

"Nah." Mr. Fletcher doesn't see the humor. "As long as he shows up, we don't stand a chance."

As long as he shows up. The words ring in my head over and over. *As long as he shows up. As long as he shows up.*

"Lola!" I say in an urgent whisper. "I got it!" I scramble down the ladder. Lola follows.

"You got what?"

"A new idea. A way to save our view. And this one is going to work."

14

Ruth-To-A's report blows up in Philly.
Mack plans to run team
as long as he's physically able.
—The Sporting News, November 1, 1934

We leave the store quickly and sprint toward home when Lola practically slams into Mrs. Sheridan, who is carrying groceries.

"Take these home, dear, and put them away. And take this bag to Mrs. Carson," she says to Lola. "I need to stop by the shop."

"I'll take that to Mrs. Carson," I say and take the smaller bag. I turn to Lola: "Meet me in the park in ten minutes. And hurry!"

"Okay," she says, and we run toward home on 20th Street.

I drop the bag off and sprint the two blocks to Reyburn Park. I enter the Funfield Rec Center and pass the swimming pool, now full of leaves and partially covered.

"Yo, Jimmy, over here," I hear from the left. "We have

98

seven; we need another." It's Santa. "We got a game of Johnny-on-the-pony started. You want in?"

"Where's your dame?" I look over and see seven guys waiting for my answer, including the Polinskis. I'm not sure which one of them said it, and choose to ignore the question.

Johnny-on-the-pony is a game where one team creates a four-person "pony" and tries to hold the other team up without toppling over. It is a brutal game, even without the Polinskis, and I tense up.

"Sure thing," I try to say casually. "But I have to be home soon." I put my army bag down and walk over to join them.

Santa, Ralph, and Matty are on my team. The four Polinski brothers are the other. Just standing near them makes me uneasy. Santa appoints himself team captain and starts giving orders.

"Shove your head into my stomach real hard and wrap your arms around my waist," he says. "Then I'll grab your back. Ralph and Matty, you two move behind us and do the same around our waists to make the pony."

We do as he says and hold tight to form an awkward arch. I hear a *ready* and brace myself. Here they come.

The first Polinski leaps on top of the arch. One Johnny on top. The second one is heavier, but we hold tight. Two Johnnies on top. I squeeze my eyes closed, hear the *ready*, and tighten up my whole body. I can hear quick feet in the dirt, a leap, and a grunt. Waves of bodies fall on top of me, roaring with laughter.

A few games later and I am officially sore. We go back and forth like that for a while, with the pony arch collapsing during the third jumper each time, until finally we change our strategy and hold a tight arch. When we don't collapse after four Polinskis/Johnnies are on top, we finally win. All eight of us lie on the ground laughing, all of us slow to get up. Beating the Polinskis feels so good, but I know not to gloat.

I limp away, still laughing. Maybe those Polinskis aren't so bad. At least the youngest one, who helped me up more than once today. Or maybe they were just too distracted to beat me up. I turn the corner and see Lola.

"What took you so long?" Lola is sitting on the edge of the metal roundabout, using her feet to circle around. I freeze and look behind me. The Polinskis are out of her sight line.

"Nothing. Just got caught up," I say.

"You kept me waiting for thirty minutes!"

"Sorry. Geez, I can't believe you're sitting there. Last time you were on this thing . . ."

"Those creeps aren't going to scare me away from anything." I'm careful not to tell her that I played a game with them. And that it ended well. I can't really believe it myself.

"Okay, you wanted me here. But you're late, and now I have to be home soon."

"I have a plan I want to run by you. A Spite Fence plan." I clear my throat and stand tall before her, pretending to start a speech.

"And you came up with this plan while we were counting hammers?" she asks, grabbing my bag.

"Yes, and it's all thanks to Bing Miller. I told you that fish was good luck."

"Oh, yeah? I thought we had to bury him before he would be lucky?" she says. I hadn't really thought about it, but she's right.

"Well, maybe this one is different. Look, if the real Bing Miller hadn't gotten released, I would not have been listening to what Pop and Mr. Fletcher were talking about. And what they said made me think of this idea. Only I'm not sure how to do it."

"Now I'm interested." She smirks and pulls her journal from my bag. "If it's good enough, I can help you figure it out. *If* it's good enough, that is."

"You heard Pop and the guys in the store talk about Shibe's lawyer, Richardson Dilworth."

"Yes, I heard them. Sounds like a rich man's name," Lola says. She stands up and brushes off her skirt. "Like a phony rich man."

We start for home. A cool wind has picked up, and dirt from the street is swirling around us. "Anyway, they also said that there is some sort of mandatory hearing next Friday, the day after Thanksgiving, between our lawyer and Shibe's lawyer."

"So?"

"So, what if we somehow stop Dilworth from making it to that hearing? It's mandatory, so if he's not there, they can't side with Shibe and Mack. Right?"

"You think they'll really just stop the wall from being built because he's not there?" When she puts it like that, I do wonder if it is that simple.

"Sure. It's mandatory. They said so. If our lawyer is there, and their lawyer isn't, then the judge has to side with us!"

"I guess. It just seems too easy. And how do you propose we prevent him from going?"

"That's the part I haven't figured out yet. They mentioned where he lives—just on the other side of the tracks."

"So, if I am a hotshot lawyer who has to make it to an important meeting near city hall, what will stop me from going?" We arrive home but aren't ready to go inside yet. I sit on the porch steps. Lola starts pacing in front of me. Her hair is swirling in the wind.

"We could sneak in and change the clocks in his house?" I suggest.

"Take his laundry from the tailor so he has nothing to wear?" she adds.

"Rig a bucket to dump water on his head when he opens the front door?" I smile at the thought.

"Put up some fake roadblocks?" She spreads her arms wide and stands in the street to demonstrate.

"Maybe we freeze water in front of his car so his wheels can't move?" I know it's ridiculous, but none of our ideas make sense.

Lola's eyes focus on a paper looping in the street. She puts her palm to her forehead and smiles. "Change the time of the meeting?"

"Change the time of the meeting!" I smile back, knowing what she is thinking. Rule #22. Why hadn't we thought of this before?

Rule #22: *Change the time of all doctor appointments when a shot is involved.*

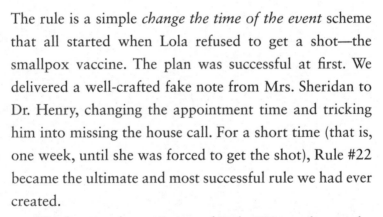

15

The rule is a simple *change the time of the event* scheme that all started when Lola refused to get a shot—the smallpox vaccine. The plan was successful at first. We delivered a well-crafted fake note from Mrs. Sheridan to Dr. Henry, changing the appointment time and tricking him into missing the house call. For a short time (that is, one week, until she was forced to get the shot), Rule #22 became the ultimate and most successful rule we had ever created.

We then used a variation of Rule #22 to play a joke on Nina and cancel what she called "the biggest date of her life," after which Nina called me "the most vile human being on the face of the earth." I would definitely call that one a success.

All it takes is some official-looking memorandum or telegram, or both, to make it work. The trick is making everything look real. We scurry off to my room and dig out my shoebox filled with the Philadelphia Athletics things I've collected, hoping that something in there will help us fake a letter.

"When is the meeting again?" Lola asks.

"They said we'd know by noon on November thirtieth. I guess sometime that morning," I reply.

"If we're caught, it might cost you batboy," Lola says, going through the box and staring at a photo of us taken on the rooftop. Shibe Park is clear as day in the background. "This is my favorite photograph, you know." She puts it back as her cheeks start to blush. "I'll be the messenger," she quickly adds.

"What? Why?"

"Look, if both of you are around the clubhouse next year, he might recognize you."

"A girl messenger?" I question. "No way. He'll know it's fake for sure."

"Girls can do anything boys can do!"

"Yes, I know. You tell me *every day*. Don't you think that Dilworth will question whether this letter is real when it's delivered by a girl?"

"I'll put my hair in a cap and wear knickers." She takes my hat and tucks her hair underneath. Not bad. "And besides, I couldn't help with the last plan because I'm a girl."

"That might work. But if he asks you a question, it'll give you away." I try to persuade her to change her mind.

"I won't open my mouth. I'll just hand it to him."

"All right," I agree. It's not worth the argument, and she will probably be fine. "Now for the memorandum."

We spend the next hour poring through different Philadelphia Athletics items. There are ticket stubs, newspaper clippings, photos, white-elephant mascot ink stamps, pins, baseball cards, a cloth pennant, and my 1929 *TIME* magazine with Jimmie Foxx on the cover. We focus on an official letter I received in the middle of the summer offering me a spot as batboy for the start of the 1935 season. There is a seal on the top of the letter and Connie Mack's signature at the bottom.

"But how do we copy this seal?" Lola ponders. I'm wondering the same thing. If all of his letters are on this paper, it will never work. Nothing here will work.

Wait! I rush to Pop's room and pull out his own memory box from the closet. His box is even bigger than mine. It reminds me of just how much baseball means to him.

I find what I'm looking for, careful to put everything back the way it was, and run back to Lola.

"This letter is from the time that section of left-field stands almost collapsed a few years ago," I explain. "And we all carried over supplies from the store in between a doubleheader. Pop and a couple of the guys were able to brace the stands for game two, until they got them fixed for real."

Dear James,

Thank you for bringing those supplies and helping in between games yesterday. We were in a real pinch and appreciate you coming out on such short notice. I'm happy to have a resource like you in the neighborhood. Please accept this token of our appreciation.

Connie Mack

The rest of the story we've heard a million times. To thank him, Connie Mack secretly sent him a whole case of Scottish Cutty Sark Whisky, which Pop then secretly shared with the whole neighborhood. All very illegal during Prohibition, which made it the perfect gift. This should work.

"I bet he can't afford gifts like that anymore," Lola says.

"Nah, this whole money thing is nonsense," I say. "Just today, I read in the paper how the Depression hasn't *really* hurt baseball. How *they* were the ones with all of the jobs. Another reason that we should stop this wall— it really is just for spite. It's not because they are losing profits."

"So, what do you think about that letter?" she says, changing the subject back and bouncing to her feet.

"I think it will work. See that ink stamp at the top?" I point to the A's mascot elephant in the right-hand corner.

"It's the same ink stamp that I have in my shoebox."

"That will work!" Lola grabs the note, and I plead with her to be careful with it.

"Yep!" she says as she stomps down the steps.

While Lola goes to work, I continue to look through my memories. I have the ticket stub from the first (and last) game I actually paid for, a wooden knot that we dug out from the wall to peek through and see inside the stadium at the ground level, an autograph from Bing Miller on the back of a napkin from Shillings on 22nd Street, and another from Mickey Cochrane on a movie ticket stub from the theater at 25th and Lehigh. There are baseball cards and newspaper articles, and a couple of photographs of Shibe Park from our rooftop.

When Lola shows back up, her smile is as wide as I've ever seen, and she's holding something behind her back.

"Back already?" I ask.

"Already? It's been an hour. Honestly, Jimmy! You are such a daydreamer!" I scramble to my feet to see what she's done.

She hands me an envelope with "Richardson Dilworth, Esq." typed on the front. I raise my eyebrows and grin. This looks real.

"Ma let me use her typewriter," she smiles. "I guess if they force me to learn to type, I may as well use it for something good."

"Esq?"

"That means lawyer," she says proudly.

The page inside looks just like Pop's note from Connie Mack. The elephant stamp looks identical.

> *Dear Mr. Dilworth,*
> *Please be advised that the hearing against*
> *the residents of 20th Street has been moved to*
> *3:00 p.m. on Friday, November 30, 1934.*
> *We look forward to hearing positive results.*
> *Thank you,*
> *Connie Mack*

"Wow!" The only real difference is that his name is typed, instead of a signature. "You are THE BEST!" I can't help but give her a big bear hug, which of course Nina sees from the hallway.

"*Awwwwwww*. Isn't that cute," she mocks. We quickly separate and whisper plans to place it into Dilworth's hands.

"If he reads it too early, he may find out it's a fake." Lola folds the note carefully into the envelope.

"I agree. You deliver it on Friday morning at his home. Before he leaves for work."

"What about school?"

"We don't *have* school the day after Thanksgiving."

"That's right!"

"What are you two scheming? I can tell you are up to

something, Jimmy Frank," Nina says from the hall.

"Nothing to concern you," I say and wait for her to leave.

"We need to figure out Dilworth's schedule," Lola whispers.

"I'll bring the binoculars."

"I'll bring my notepad."

"Let's meet outside tomorrow at seven a.m. sharp," I suggest.

"You're going to get up that early? Pinky swear." She hooks her pinky into mine.

"Pinky swear. I'll be up. Surveillance tomorrow. Deliver it Friday. This is gonna work, Lola. I just know it."

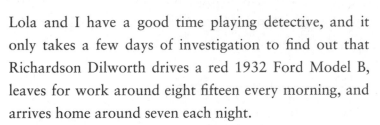

Lola and I have a good time playing detective, and it only takes a few days of investigation to find out that Richardson Dilworth drives a red 1932 Ford Model B, leaves for work around eight fifteen every morning, and arrives home around seven each night.

It's not until Tuesday that I start to panic.

"What if it doesn't work? What then?" Lola and I are on the roof, prepping it for the winter. We dig the tulip bulbs out of the flowerpots and put a tarp over the bleachers.

"Calm down. There is no reason for him to question it." Lola is just as nervous as I am, but she is doing a good job of pretending that she is the opposite.

"And besides, I've got my performance down just right." She tucks her hair in the hat and walks around like she's a boy, pretending to chew gum and spit. She even swears one time and we both giggle.

"You're good," I say truthfully. "I just wish we had a backup plan in case this doesn't work."

"One thing at a time, Jimmy. If we can't fake him out, all we can do is hope that he runs out of gas." She smiles and continues with her *I-can-act-like-a-boy* show. But all I can think of is what she just said.

"Hey, that's actually a good idea, too. How can we make sure Richardson Dilworth's car runs out of gas?" I say aloud.

"Jimmy! One thing at a time!"

"I just think that's a good idea, too," I say. "But you're right."

"Hey, Jimmy Frank," I hear from below, followed by a whistle. Santa, Ralph, and Matty wave me down for a game of half-ball. Lola and I peek down and see the Polinski brothers not far behind.

"I gotta go," I say to Lola, hurrying to the back ladder and waving goodbye.

"What's your hurry?"

"Just need to see someone about something."

"Yeah, yeah," she says. Her shoulder slumps and she pretends to spit one last time. "Hey—stay away from them. Rule #19."

A guilty pit forms in my stomach as I make my way down. Rule #19: *Stay away from the four Polinski brothers at all costs.*

112

I meet the three of them out front at the same time that the Polinskis join the group. I look up, relieved that Lola doesn't see me with them, but I still cross the street to be out of view.

"How you guys doin'?" I ask the brothers.

"Pretty good," the youngest one replies. Matty crinkles his forehead, and I shrug my shoulders. None of the other brothers answers.

Two games of half-ball and one Johnny-on-the-pony later and we're all making our way home. I'm clenching my stomach after falling one too many times—or maybe it's my nerves. *All we can do is hope that he runs out of gas* rings in my head. I take a deep breath. Now is my chance. This backup plan could work.

I keep behind and watch the brothers start to walk home. One of the middle brothers lags behind, and I make my way across the street to catch up with him.

"Hey, Polinski," I say, but only a little louder than my regular voice. He doesn't turn around.

"POLINSKI!" I say, quite a bit louder than I expected. The adults chatting across the street look over to me, probably wondering why anyone in their right mind would knowingly try to have a conversation with any of the Polinski brothers.

"This better be good or I'll kick your *ass*." His arms are crossed, and his face contorts into a scowl. He's a few inches shorter than me, but I believe him.

I clear my throat. "Um, I was wondering if you and

your brothers might want to help me with something."

He starts to walk away.

"You'll get free stuff out of it." He stops in his tracks.

"What do you need, and be quick about it. The old lady's got ham and mash waiting for me."

"Oh. I, uh, need to pull some gas from a car over on 26th Street," I say uneasily, quickly regretting this decision.

"Yeah, why?"

"Well, I'm trying to stop someone from going somewhere." I stumble over every word. I sound pathetic.

He snickers. "And your best plan is to take his gas? Just slash his tires and be done with it."

"Well," I clear my throat again. "I'm not really comfortable with that, so I'm going to try to siphon the gas."

"All right. What's in it for us?"

"Well, I guess we'll need a hose and a gas can. I'll pick them up new from the store and you guys can have them when we are through."

"And the gas?"

I wasn't prepared for this. The plan came about so quickly in my head that I didn't have a great answer.

"I'm planning on just leaving the gas on his back stoop. Kind of like a prank." I'm forcing a cheerful voice. "Siphon, not steal. Wouldn't that be funny?" I sound like an idiot.

"Then how do we get the can?"

"Oh, I . . ."

114

I'm not prepared for the curse words that now come out of his mouth. Something like: *You can't be serious, Jimmy Frank. You want us to risk gettin' caught just because you're too much of a wimp? Steal the gas, only not to steal it? You are a joke, your idea is a joke, and your girlfriend is a joke. Now get out of my way before you regret it.* Only *these* words are littered with words that start with *A* and *S* and even a few that start with *F*.

"Um, I . . ."

"*Um, I,*" he sneers. "Get a life, Jimmy Frank. Or maybe get your girlfriend to help you."

Lola is walking toward us. I look back to the Polinski brother, and he's already a block away.

"You did *what?*" Lola says after I explain.

I don't answer and just stare at the sidewalk, trying not to step on the cracks.

"Maybe it was *you* who got struck in the head instead of Jimmie Foxx!" She throws her hands in the air. "Did you forget all about Rule #19?"

"You know I can't stay away from them. We go to the *same* school and we live in the *same* neighborhood. And besides, they've been all right the last couple of weeks."

She squints her eyes and burns a gaze into my head.

"What? One game on a playground and suddenly you're all chummy?"

"No. I just thought they could do it. And then I'm not involved."

"And you don't see how dangerous that is? They get

115

caught, you get caught. Even if you're not there."

"Nobody will believe that I'm involved with them," I reply.

"And then you'll spend the rest of your life running from them! And I thought we were in this together. How could you do that without me?"

I don't say anything and she presses on. "Then tell me, when did your little ideas become so illegal?"

"You're not such an angel, Lola, so stop acting like it. You sneak into the ballpark. You're going to deliver a fake letter on Friday."

"Those things aren't throw-you-in-jail illegal. They don't harm anything. You know that."

"See, that's the thing." I look up. "It's not illegal! It wouldn't be *stealing* his gas, just *hiding* his gas. He can put the gas back in the car. Just put it right back in!" I realize that I'm stepping on several cracks now and feel irritated.

"Calm down, Jimmy. I have a right to be upset. You don't."

"I can be tough and mean like those kids, you know."

"Why would you want to be?" She stops in her tracks.

"I'm not so good, Lola." My voice is starting to rise. "I'm sick of hiding from them all the time. I'm sick of being the nice kid all the time. And I'm sick of doing the right thing. What do I get? I get to hide in shadows. I get to scrounge for every penny. I get to watch a wall built right in front of my window."

116

"You'd never have done something like that without me before," she says.

"Well nothing came of it, anyway." I try to break the tension by changing the subject. "Hey, did you hear that Jimmie Foxx signed a three-year contract?"

No response.

"He's staying with the A's. That's great news for us." I try again.

Still no response.

"And he's playing catcher," I add, knowing she'll react.

"Sure. Okay. He's going from first base to catcher. That's ridiculous. Now you are just trying to see if I'm paying attention, Jimmy. I *am* paying attention to you. I *always* pay attention to you. I'm just *choosing* not to respond."

"Honest, Lola! See—here," I say as I pull out the paper. She reads as we make our way into Reyburn Park.

"That's really something. Too bad you can't bring him warm pie from jail." And with that, we turn the corner and almost slam right into the four Polinski brothers.

"Hey Frank, I hear you need someone to do your dirty work for you," the oldest Polinski says, staring at Lola. She steps forward and opens her mouth to say something, but I cut her off.

"Nah," I say uneasily. "It was just an idea. I'll do it on my own."

"Too late, dimwit. We sure could use a gas can," he says, and the middle brothers step forward. "But leave

117

your girlfriend at home."

Lola mumbles something under her breath, and the oldest Polinski starts moving toward her. I step in between.

"Sure guys. Um, Thanksgiving night. Let's talk about it at school tomorrow," I quickly say. I can feel Lola's eyes burning in the back of my head as I turn to leave.

"You better come through, Frank."

"Or what?" Lola says, and I stop in my tracks, holding my breath. The oldest Polinski comes within an inch of her face and she stands her ground.

"You don't wanna know."

17

"I'm gonna make a scene." She says it with that sort of face that tells me I can't change her mind. But I still try.

"Come on, Lola. It's Thanksgiving night. Give it a chance," I say.

We sit on the stoop of St. Columba under the stained-glass window, waiting for the evening to take shape.

"I can't believe you are doing this," she says.

"I know. I can't believe it either. I'm so dumb," I reply.

"Yep."

"Yep."

"Maybe it's a sign, meeting here." Lola points to the stained-glass window. "It's like he's telling you not to go." We both stare at the large, round, glass window with Jesus in the center; its soft colors are barely glimmering in the low light from the gas streetlamps. He's looking right down on us. As usual, I try to catch his eye, with no luck.

"Nah, he's telling us to fight for what we believe."

"By committing a sin?"

"Maybe I'm that dove in the corner. Flying free."

"You are not free while the Polinskis are in control," she says. "Where's that money from, anyway?"

"What money?"

"For the gas can. And the hose." She points to the box of supplies on the step.

"I made it an IOU from a Mr. Miller at the store. Figured Bing Miller needs to give me a whole lot of luck right about now. The IOU will give me some time to pay the money back."

"How much?" she asks.

"Thirty-seven cents for the gas can, and twenty cents for the piece of hose," I reply. "I'll go down to the next Eagles game and park some cars to make it back."

"So, you have it all figured out?"

"Look, I made a mistake, but it's too late now. Can't you just wish me luck?"

"Try to catch his eye again." She points to the stained glass. "Maybe he can bring you luck."

"I already tried."

"It's not too late," she says in frustration and buries her head in her hands.

"Listen, all they need is for me to be a lookout. I'll barely do anything. And it's happening tonight because nobody will be around on Thanksgiving. If that telegram doesn't work tomorrow morning, this is a great backup plan. When he tries to start his car, it will be out of gas." I pause, and there is an uncomfortable silence. "It's brilliant, really."

"Brilliant," she replies flatly.

"Lola, please don't embarrass me."

"Embarrass you! That's better than me having to explain to your parents *why* they have to pay a fine when you're in jail," she says.

"That's not fair! You'll say anything right now to stop me."

"You're right, Jimmy! I'll say and I'll do anything! Because of Rule #12: *Jimmy and Lola will always be best friends forever*. Because it's Thanksgiving!"

"Some Thanksgiving. We didn't even have a decent meal. Tomato gravy and biscuits. You didn't either! What did you have, potato soup?" I say bitterly.

"Exactly!" she says. "Do you want to be the one to make it worse? Do you want to be the one to ruin Thanksgiving?"

I put my hands to my ears, but she doesn't let up.

"Honestly Jimmy, tomorrow is the plan. Rule #22 is the plan. Change the time of the meeting is the plan! None of that will happen if you are caught doing this tonight."

"That won't happen." My voice is a little weak, and again, I know that she is right.

"Oh, come *on*! It's like I'm stuck in the middle of one of your daydreams and can't find my way out! Do you really think the Polinskis will do it just for fun?

Do you really think they'll say, 'Okay, Jimmy. We've taken all the gas out of the car so that Dilworth can't drive to his court hearing. Now let's make sure we return the gas.' And then they'll all beg to be the ones to leave the gas can safely by Dilworth's back door." Her face is bright red. "They don't care. They are going to take that gas and sell it. It's not a prank. It's stealing, and it was your idea."

"No. It's just a prank. If they steal it, that's their idea." I'm saying the words, but I know she's right. "And anyway, I can't turn back now." We see them coming toward the church. A moment later, the oldest takes the gas can and hose from the box.

"What's she doing here?" one of the brothers sneers.

"She's just leaving." My eyes plead with Lola to go quietly, but I wish I had said I was leaving. Her head and shoulders drop just enough for me to know—she was hoping I'd come. I want to turn back time. I open my mouth to tell her to stop, but nothing comes out.

She walks away, motioning for me to follow one final time. I look from her, to the brothers, and back.

"Come with me, Jimmy," she says from the corner.

I turn away, joining the Polinskis as we start toward Dilworth's house.

18

The four brothers look tattered and walk with a sort of tough-guy strut. As I join them, with my good posture and clean knickers and warm coat, I look like the odd man out. I pull out my tucked-in shirt, slump my shoulders, and awkwardly walk beside them. Halfway there, the youngest brother tugs at my coat.

"*Why are you doing this?*" he whispers with an urgency that surprises me.

"What?" I whisper back. He rolls his eyes.

"Look, just keep your head down," he says quietly. "And if it gets bad—*run.*" I give him a nod and continue to look forward. Why is he trying to help me?

"It's that one," I say and point to the red car three houses away. I look down at my finger and realize it's shaking. I immediately put my hand in my pocket.

"Yowzer, she's a beaut. You stay here and keep a

lookout," one of them says to me. I watch as they all crouch and surround the car. It's freezing, but sweat has formed on the back of my neck. "And quit acting so guilty. You'll get us all caught."

The wind is rattling a metal trash can lid and whipping a piece of newspaper down the street. It scrapes the ground with a *swish* every few seconds. My heart leaps out of my chest at the noise each time.

I notice an older lady on her porch take an interest in the brothers, and I tuck my face into my sweater so she doesn't recognize me. The sweat is now starting to form on my brow, and my knees begin to shake. I slide closer to the edge of the street behind a black convertible.

That's when I hear her yelling for me.

"Hey, Jimmy!"

I pretend not to hear Lola's voice, and turn my back to where I think she is walking. The oldest Polinski peeks out from behind the car and motions for me. I creep up, even though my legs are wobbling uncontrollably.

"You go shut her up. You hear me? Get her out of here, Jimmy Frank."

Before I know it, Lola is standing next to me, out of breath.

"Jimmy's Ma is asking for him. I have strict instructions to come home with him."

"Listen Frank, you got us out here, dragging this stuff." The oldest Polinski lifts the can and hose. "Now let's do this."

Lola is pulling my arm as she starts to cross the street. The four brothers eye one another.

"Don't worry about it, Jimmy," another brother says. "We'll take care of it, Buddy. And thanks for these." He points to the supplies.

"Okay, just leave the gas on his stoop. Promise?" I say in a loud whisper.

"Sure," he turns away. A couple of them laugh.

"Sounds great!" I say desperately. They all stop what they are doing and stare.

"*Go,*" the youngest brother silently mouths to us. Lola and I turn our back to the Polinskis.

"Move quickly," Lola urges. "Trust me."

We turn the corner and immediately see a police officer heading in our direction.

"Oh my God," I say under my breath.

"Keep calm," Lola whispers. "Follow my lead."

She pulls me closer, hooks her arm into mine, and leans her head on my shoulder. She giggles a little and starts talking like she's in the middle of a story.

"And then Gram said *those people are nuts,* and we all laughed. She tells the best stories! Then we had apple pie for dessert with real whipped cream and . . ."

She keeps going as he passes, and again does a nice job of acting like a lovestruck teenager, out for a stroll after Thanksgiving dinner.

A block later, she lets go and crosses her arms.

"You owe me one," she says coldly.

125

"Where did he come from?"

"I saw him walking this direction up on 22nd Street, so I doubled around the block and sprinted all the way to you. I didn't think I was going to make it to you in time."

"So, you didn't call him?"

"*What?* Do you really think I would do that!"

"No. Of course not," I say quietly, shaking my head. "Thank you. Thank you. Thank you." I bury my face in my sweaty palms. "What was I thinking?"

"You *weren't* thinking," she snaps.

"Do you think they'll be caught?" I glance back.

"Yes." She says this so matter-of-factly, and I know she's right.

"I should be there. They'll kill me." I look back to see the officer has turned the corner and is heading directly for them.

"Then you would have been in jail too. Period."

"They're really going to kill me. They are going to beat me to a pulp," I say, staring at my feet. My stomach lurches, and I feel a sudden urge to vomit.

"Hold on." I pause and sit on a stoop. "Just give me a second." I take deep breaths as Lola stands before me, arms crossed.

"You can catch your breath at home," she says, tapping her foot.

"Now I've gone and done it. You think they'll tell the cops about me?"

"Probably, but like you said before, nobody will believe them. They're caught doing something bad every day."

"I'll never have another moment of peace."

"You will if they are in jail."

"Oh, God. If they say my name, the cops will come to my house and ask questions."

"Let's just worry about what we can—and that's the original plan. Change the time of Dilworth's meeting," she says. "Now let's get going." She takes my hands and pulls me up.

"You still want to do that with me?"

"Of course I do."

"I'm sorry, Lola."

"I know."

Again she hooks her arm in mine.

"I'm really lucky to have you," I say awkwardly.

"Rule #12. Best friends," she replies, and gives me a reassuring smile as we start for home.

19

Mack is using the Japanese scene to break Jimmie Foxx in as a catcher, the position he is to play next season . . .
—The Sporting News, November 22, 1934

Between the tensions the night before and the sleepless night, I leave for the letter-delivery exhausted. I have no idea if the gas-stealing Polinskis pulled it off, or if they were caught. I'm careful not to bring it up.

"Ready?" I say as we walk down the porch steps.

"Sure," Lola replies in a low voice. There is no enthusiasm today. None of the pre-plan nervous excitement that we felt on the Knothole Gang day. Our mission feels more like a chore than a thrilling save-the-neighborhood scheme.

We walk the five blocks to 26th Street completely silent, passing cars and watching cold-morning steam rise from the rows of rooftops. Just before we turn down the street, Lola ducks into a shadow and quickly pulls down her skirt, revealing her brother's knickers underneath. I give her my coat and A's ball cap, and she tucks her hair in.

128

As planned, we arrive at seven thirty a.m. sharp, with Lola looking so much like a boy that it's the least of my worries.

"Good luck," I whisper and give her shoulder a squeeze. I'm nervous, but I put the worry aside and hide around the corner, peeking quietly as Lola stands on the porch and knocks on the door.

It seems to take forever, and she glances back at me. His car is still here, so why isn't he answering? I wonder if the gas has indeed been stolen, and maybe he caught a ride with someone else. She starts to turn away from the door when it begins to open.

I crouch lower and can barely see as she hands Richardson Dilworth the letter and has him sign a clipboard that I borrowed from the store. He hands her a tip, and she nods. As planned, she didn't utter a word.

Lola leaves the porch and rounds the corner. We run down the street giggling. She takes her cap off and lets her long brown hair fall past her shoulders. Her eyes and smile are both wide, and we are floating on air. What a difference ten minutes can make.

"Finally, something worked!" I slow down to catch my breath.

"I can't believe it! He didn't even look up. He had no idea I was a girl!"

"You were great. You should dress like a boy more often."

"Well, this getup sure is more comfortable than my dresses." We both almost double over laughing.

"A whole *dollar*!" she exclaims, holding it up.

"What!" I grab it from her and examine it. "Wow, he must be really rich."

"You should have seen the inside of his house. Plush velvet sofas, thick oriental rugs, a Tiffany lamp on the table. I wonder what the rest of the house looks like."

"Maybe I should be a lawyer," I say dreamily.

"First things first," she says as she takes back the bill. "You can pay back the store with this, and we'll still have forty-three cents change."

"Jimmie Foxx is the only other person I ever saw tip one whole dollar," I say.

"I'm going to be that rich one day," Lola says. "And I'm going to tip kids a dollar, too."

"I'll be your business partner."

"You better be!"

"So, you're not mad at me anymore? From last night?"

"I can never stay mad at you, Jimmy! Just don't be a dummy anymore. Hey, let's go to Doc Hoffman's for some hot cocoa."

"Yeah?"

"Well I can't give this money to Ma. She'll wonder where it came from, and I can't lie to her," she says.

"Sounds like a good reason to me."

We walk the few blocks to the diner and grab a booth, ordering two hot chocolates with extra whipped cream.

"Ten cents each," Lola says and starts counting on her fingers. "So, that's fifty-seven cents to pay back to the store, twenty cents for hot cocoa, and a five-cent tip." She closes her eyes to concentrate. "We'll have eighteen cents left over."

"Not bad!"

"Let's keep it in your army bag for a rainy day," she says.

"Or maybe penny candy?"

Moments later, they arrive—two steaming mugs filled with rich, sweet chocolate, and mounds of white cream. Lola's grin is so wide, and we both grab at the spoons in anticipation. I can hardly believe our luck.

"It worked, you know," I say. "He's going to miss the meeting *and* we have hot cocoa as a reward."

"I don't remember the last time I had something like this," she says. I can barely see her eyes over the big mug and the whipped cream on her nose.

Silence falls between us as we drink. We both stare out the window at the activity. The window has become hazy around the edges as the warm diner meets the outdoor temperature. There is steam coming from the street vents. With the holiday, there are only a few cars on the road, a handful of ladies bundled in coats and hats, and a couple of kids lugging books from the library a few doors down. We hear a *ding,* and moments later the trolley comes along, dropping riders off and picking a few up.

Lola's eyes start to droop at the mundane hustle and bustle, and she rests her head on the table.

"I didn't really sleep at all last night," she says.

"Me either." Thirty minutes in a warm diner and any adrenaline we had is long gone.

"So, how do we know if Dilworth leaves?" she finally says, sitting up and rubbing her face.

"I'll go back around ten o'clock to see if his car is gone."

"Okay. Ring the Bingle and I'll come along." She pauses. "Want to go down to Reyburn Park? See if anyone heard about the Polinskis?"

I shrug my shoulders and stare out the window again. Lola decides to drop the subject and we sit quietly, finishing our hot chocolate.

We walk home in silence and part ways, both exhausted. My mind is once again jumbled and uneasy. I worry about the Polinskis, and whether Rule #22 will work, and how we can find out about the hearing today. But most of all, I worry about the wall. I picture it as I walk along the street, craning my head up to try and guess how tall it will be. Will it block out all the sun?

"Morning, son," Pop says when I open the front door. I jump back, startled. He and Nina are standing in the living room as if they've been waiting.

"You scared me!"

"Sorry about that," Pop forces a smile. "Where did you go off to so early today?"

"Just around," I reply truthfully. "Where's Ma?"

"Ma's out working," Pop says.

"What?"

"Yes, Ma's down at the Sheridan's store. They landed a Christmas order and needed an extra person to embroider. She's got a knack for that sort of thing," Pop says. "We really can use the money, Jimmy." He wrings his hands together and I feel even more guilty. We had a whole dollar that I spent on hot cocoa and supplies that are now in the Polinskis' hands. Not to mention the extra eighteen cents burning a hole in my army bag.

"Well, that's good then. Besides, Ma's never really gone to work except at the hardware store," I say. That's when I notice Nina's eyes are puffy and red again.

"What's wrong?" She doesn't answer and blows her nose in Pop's handkerchief.

"The job over at The Hop Inn fell through," Pop says. He rubs her back, and she buries her head in his chest.

"If I don't find a job soon, I'm going to have to drop out of school," she blubbers.

"Now, now. I'm not going to let that happen," he tries to reassure her.

"You said it yourself!" she wails.

"Let's try our other plan first. If you work in the store every day after school, that will give me a chance to start back up my handyman work. You know that kept us afloat long before we opened."

"I can help out after school, too," I jump in.

"We are going to count on that." Pop smiles and puts his arms around both of us.

"Or should I find a job? Maybe the pharmacist will

133

give me some work. I can do more deliveries for him," I offer.

"Maybe, son. Let's take it one day at a time."

"And they'll pay me as batboy next year."

"Good. For now, we all just need to stick together. Take these hiccups one at a time. We should have had a better Thanksgiving. You know, there really is a lot to be thankful for," he says. "We have a roof over our heads. We have a healthy family. We have a lot more than others."

"But will we still have all of this if I can't find work?" Nina whispers. I suddenly feel ashamed for not seeing the pressure she's been under. Pop puts his hands on both of her shoulders.

"One day at a time, okay?" he says. She nods her head in agreement, her lip still quivering. "I sure would like to bring some joy into this house right now," he adds.

"Maybe we can have a nice meal tonight," Nina says, dabbing her eyes one more time. Pop and I look at each other, not used to her soft tone.

"When will Ma be home?" I ask.

"Not until later. Sure would be nice to surprise her." Pop stands up with a sudden burst of energy. "We have six hours before she's home. That's six hours to clean the house, wash the windows, change the sheets, do the laundry, and make supper."

Nina and I stare at each other for a moment, both smirking. Pop's sudden change in mood is jarring.

"Run down to the corner and pick up some noodles. We're makin' lasagna." Nina glances over at me and I shrug my shoulders.

We burst into action like we are little kids again.

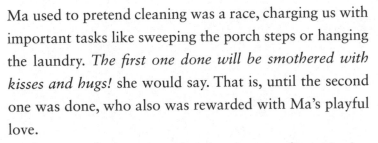

20

Ma used to pretend cleaning was a race, charging us with important tasks like sweeping the porch steps or hanging the laundry. *The first one done will be smothered with kisses and hugs!* she would say. That is, until the second one was done, who also was rewarded with Ma's playful love.

I run to the basement for cleaning supplies, tripping on Ma's bag of tulip bulbs and knocking over an ironing board along the way. Nina starts for upstairs.

We finish each room with a sense of pride, looking at our work from the door before moving on to the next one. I pull on the Bingle. Before long, Lola comes in the house to find me, and I fill her in.

"Your Ma's at our shop? I'll go down and see if they need my help," she says.

"Okay," I say and look back for Nina, who is not paying attention. I whisper: "On the way can you go see about Dilworth's car? And can I give Nina the extra change from today for the lasagna?"

"Sure!" she says with a big smile.

I quietly slip Nina the eighteen cents, saving the final change to pay back the store for the gas can and hose.

"Hey, where did you find this?" she asks.

"Saved it from tips," I say, hoping for no follow-up questions. That seems to satisfy her, and she pockets it.

"I'll be back in a few minutes, Pop," she yells before heading out the door. In no time, I finish the upstairs and start cleaning on the first level. Four hours to go.

"We couldn't afford the good meat." Nina hurries back in and unloads everything from the corner store onto the table. "But I was able to buy a few sausage links."

"I'm surprised we had enough for even that!" Pop says, grabbing the canvas bag to see for himself. Nina and I give each other a knowing look. At least something good has come out of the Dilworth delivery this morning.

Pop takes the two feet of sausage, and he jokingly barks orders to Nina like a chef. He is surprising in the kitchen, moving quickly and generally knowing what to do and when to do it.

"Look at you!" Nina says.

"Your nana Millie taught me how to cook. Bet you didn't know that with Ma being so good in the kitchen.

I certainly can hold my own."

Lola returns and waves for me to come out to the porch.

"Dilworth's car is still in the same spot as it was this morning," she whispers.

"Wow, this might work! Any word on the Polinskis?"

"No," she replies. "I saw Ralph and Matty, but they didn't mention anything."

"Okay then." I try not to show it bothers me. "Are you heading back to the store?"

"No. They have an assembly line going and I'll be in the way at this point. Can I stay here and help?"

"Yes!" We both grin from ear to ear.

The distraction of the day is a welcome relief. Nina puts on the radio, and eventually I'm skipping around to Fats Waller and "Honeysuckle Rose," broom in hand.

Nina and Pop are in the kitchen working on the lasagna. Whenever Nina tries to guide him—*"use the brown potholders, that green potholder is too thin"* or *"take the sausage out of the casing first"* or *"try layering the noodles in the other direction"*—he says something about having it covered and not to worry.

I notice that she is secretly changing the measurements and the order of his layers, putting in half the cheese or extra parsley.

While they are cooking, Lola and I are charged with cleaning the kitchen floor.

"I want to be able to eat off it," Pop says, while tomato

and sausage grease splatter with every movement. We each take a corner farthest from the chaos and carefully use a rag to rinse and wipe, rinse and wipe, rinse and wipe. I hum to the radio as I clean the floor.

"Today feels more like Thanksgiving," I say to Lola, who nods her head.

Pop eventually pours an extra can of tomato gravy over the finished product, making the whole pan of noodles and cheese and meat swim in the sauce. Nina crinkles her nose, but I can't wait for this meal. Ma's tomato gravy is the best, and the hot summer provided us with some sweet juicy tomatoes. I'd eat it straight from the jar with a spoon, if Ma would let me.

Once they are completely done with the cooking, we are able to clean the floor around the stove. This is a harder job. Grease and dirt are coating the floor, and before I know it, my arms are sore and the muscles are throbbing.

"Maybe this will build some muscle so you can actually *play* baseball instead of just watching," Lola jabs.

"Like this?" My rag hits her hard in the face, and we are soon splashing water and slipping over each other in a fit of laughter.

"That's enough, you two," Pop says. "Let's finish up. She'll be home soon."

The next half hour is abuzz with the four of us rushing around the house. Nina quickly takes over.

"Jimmy, pick up leftover laundry and bring it to the

basement. Lola, help me with these dirty pans. Pop . . ."

Pop is at the radio. He starts to croon along with Cole Porter before Nina cuts him off.

"*Pop!* Help dry these dishes!"

He turns up the music and heads to the kitchen. We finish with moments to spare.

"Let's get cleaned up," Pop says. Lola rushes next door to wash, and we stomp upstairs. On the way up, I look at the kitchen floor. It sparkles like new.

"Here she comes!" Nina yells. I look out my bedroom window. Ma is at the end of the street bundled up, head down, and trying to avoid the wind. It's fighting her as she makes her way. I ring the Bingle and hurry downstairs, just as Lola rushes back in the front door.

We are giddy as we line up to greet her, Nina and Pop on one side, me and Lola on the other. I'm excited. I'm happy that Lola is here to help. And I think I have the best pop in the world. Time spent with Pop is usually always at the store. This is special.

Ma walks in, and her eyes light up immediately.

"Oh my!" she says over and over. Pop sweeps her off her feet with a long kiss and hug, and Nina blushes as she replaces Ma's shoes with slippers. I love it when Ma and Pop hug and kiss. They sit on the sofa, her feet resting on his legs.

"Well, this certainly is a nice surprise," she says, looking at all of us.

"We weren't quite satisfied with Thanksgiving," Pop says. "Thought we'd have another go at it."

"Really?" Her eyes begin to glisten. "How special."

"And we cleaned the house!" I blurt out. Lola shoves my shoulder.

"Is that so? All four of you? I am one lucky lady." She looks around quite satisfied. "Thank you."

She leans on Pop's shoulder. The smell of garlic and onions and sausage fills the air, and the music continues to play.

"I'm starving," she finally says with a genuine smile. "What, pray tell, have you made for me?"

"What do you think?" he asks.

"Pop and I made lasagna," Nina says before Ma even has a chance to answer. She proudly grins from ear to ear.

"Lasagna?" Ma bolts upright. "But how?"

"No worries," Pop cuts her off and kisses her again.

Nina finishes setting the table, and Lola steadies me as I reach high in the cupboard for candles. It's getting dark and that seems like the right thing to do. I find two candles—one short, stubby, and fat, and one long and slender.

Lola says goodbye and gives Ma a hug.

"Young lady, you aren't going anywhere! You helped make this happen, dear."

"Thank you, Ms. Frances. I'd love to stay," Lola replies more formally than usual. Ma squeezes her.

141

"And besides, you are part of this family. There will always be a seat for you at our table. Nina, would you please set another place?"

Nina nudges me and smiles. I think she's going to poke fun, but she just says that it's time to sit.

Nina, Lola, and Ma are across from me at the table laughing, and Pop is taking the pan out of the oven when I see a fast movement out of the corner of my eye, followed by a loud *thump*. We all quickly turn to Pop.

I first see the green potholder in Pop's right hand—the one that's too thin—and the brown one in his left. From the potholders, I look down, toward the open oven. The pan must have been too hot, and Pop dropped it back onto the oven rack. I sigh with relief at what could have been a lasagna disaster.

"That sure was close," Pop says to nobody in particular. He looks over at us and pretends to wipe his brow with the potholder. That's when we hear the sound.

"The rack!" Nina cries, but it's too late. That thump of the heavy lasagna pan proves too much for the oven rack. It tips slowly, just enough for the pan to drop onto the open oven door.

"Goodness!" Ma says, her hand coming to her chest as she breathes deeply. Pop grins nervously, and Lola and I start to laugh.

But the path of the lasagna isn't over. Pop starts to reach down when—*No! No! No!*

He sees it before any of us.

142

The old oven door, not meant to hold a heavy-loaded pan, gives way and slants to the ground. The entire meal slides down and skids across the kitchen, stopping right in the center of the room. Pop lunges for it, but it all happens too fast.

The entire rectangle of noodles and cheese and sausage sloshes out of the pan and onto the floor.

We all stare at the scene. A sloppy block of red and brown and white on the floor, followed by a dirty pan, a slanted oven door, a tilted oven rack, and Pop, whose mouth hangs open. He stands there with the brown mitt on his right hand, and the green mitt on his left.

I wanted to laugh. *Don't laugh.* I pinch myself and avoid looking into Lola's eyes. What is she thinking? What is Pop thinking? Poor Pop. Poor Ma. Suddenly, I want to cry. *Don't cry.*

Ma takes her eyes away from the incredible scene and calmly looks at me. "You say you scrubbed the floor today?"

"Yes, Ma. We both did." I motion toward Lola. "Clean enough to eat off of," I say without thinking and quickly wish I could shove the words right back in my mouth.

Ma smiles. "Then that's exactly what we'll do."

We sit frozen and watch Ma gather the forks and napkins and seat herself on the floor. Nina grabs the candles and nudges me, and we all spring to life. Lola sits next to me, grinning from ear to ear. Pop whispers something to Ma, and they both giggle like school kids.

143

"Come on now, let's say our words," she says, taking my hand and Nina's. I take Lola's in mine, and she looks at me and gives me a squeeze.

Together, we sit on the floor in a circle around our dinner.

"Dear Lord," Ma prays. "Thank you for my family, and thank you for this wonderful meal. It's one of the best nights of my life."

"Amen!" we say loudly. We take our forks and dig in, and I make a note in my head to create a rule about this very soon.

21

The wall will be built high enough to put the outlaw stands on the roofs of Twentieth street dwellings out of business. This has been a sore spot with the A's for years.
—The Sporting News, December 20, 1934

"Bad news, son."

Pop's voice startles me, and my eyes jolt open. He is standing over me with his hands in his pockets and takes a seat at the edge of the bed. What day is today? Am I late for school?

Then I remember the events of the days before. Polinskis. Dilworth. Cops. Hot cocoa. Lasagna. The hearing.

"The hearing?" I ask. Pop nods, and I sit up.

"Mr. O'Connor came over after you went to bed. We lost."

"What? That can't be!" I say.

"They had a really good lawyer. We knew it would be a long shot, anyway." There is a long pause. "They'll build it before next season begins."

145

"But wait! Didn't their lawyer miss the hearing? Didn't he think it was at a different time? Did he have gas in his car? I thought that if they didn't have a lawyer there, the judge would side with us. *Didn't that happen?*"

I realize how crazy I sound, but I stare at him, my eyes pleading for an answer. The corners of his mouth curl up a bit.

"He was at the hearing. He didn't miss it." Pop rises from the bed and stands above me, arms crossed.

"Really? Are you certain?"

"I'm certain. Is there anything you want to tell me?"

"No, Pop," I reply.

"Really? Because O'Connor heard something about a prank played on their lawyer."

"Prank?" I say uneasily.

"Thought the hearing time had been changed. You wouldn't know anything about that, would you?"

"No." I flop back on my pillow so he can't see my face.

"If you change your mind, I'll be at the store doing inventory," he says.

"But I just did that," I snap.

"Well, we may have had a theft. I need to make sure nothing else is missing," he says. I shoot up to a sitting position.

"Why do you think that?"

"The police dropped off an empty gas can they found in the street. Had our stamp on the bottom."

146

"A gas can? Who do they think stole it? Where was it?" I spew the questions quickly, and Pop crosses his arms.

"James Frances, is there something you need to say to me right now?" he says firmly.

"No, Pop. Nothing." I bury my head in my hands and wait for him to leave.

A few minutes later, I hear the Bingle.

"I guess the Polinskis weren't caught," Lola says when I meet her on the rooftop. "The police would have told your father that."

"No. They didn't get caught. And I'm sick and tired of worrying about them. We lost the hearing. That's what we should focus on."

"But Jimmy, they're out roaming the streets right now," she says uneasily.

"There's got to be something we can do."

"Maybe try to talk to them in school? Smooth things over while there's an adult around," she says.

"I'm not talking about the Polinski brothers. Can you just focus on the Spite Fence for a minute?"

"It's just that—well, don't you think you *should* focus on more pressing matters?"

"What could be more pressing than the Spite Fence?" I snap.

"Um, maybe that the Polinskis are probably out for you again? You can't ignore it!"

"I'm not, Lola! But they aren't up here on this rooftop.

147

Can't we forget them for ten minutes?"

"It just seems like you are focusing all of your energy on a lost cause. You'll have to face it sooner or later. That wall is happening."

"So, you're giving up."

"I'm smart enough to know when we've lost," she says, picking up her journal to write something. "And you should be making plans to settle this Polinski thing. No more plans to fix the wall."

"I'll figure out what to do," I say.

"About the Polinskis or the Spite Fence?"

"I'm not going to stop!" I raise my voice at her and point to right field. "That wall isn't even up yet!"

"Quit taking everything out on me! Yesterday was so much fun. Can't we just move on?" Lola asks.

"Sure," I reply sharply. "Look, I gotta go."

"Where?"

"Just have some things to do."

"Okay. Maybe the park later?" she asks.

"I don't know. I might have to help Pop with the inventory," I say. I know that I am being terrible and can barely look in her direction.

"Yeah. Well, I have to help at the shop, too," she says. I can't tell if she is telling the truth. We part ways, each going down our skylights.

I return to my room and climb back into bed. The Polinskis are on the loose. The police are involved. We lost the hearing. We all need to bring in more money. Lola doesn't understand me.

I pull the covers over my head.

The Bingle doesn't ring once all weekend.

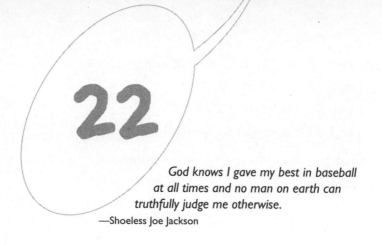

*God knows I gave my best in baseball
at all times and no man on earth can
truthfully judge me otherwise.*
—Shoeless Joe Jackson

I wrap my afghan around my shoulders and hop to the window. Monday morning brings a surprise, razor-thin blanket of snow, early, and the first of the season. There is only one person on the dark street so far today. He slips but doesn't fall, steadying himself with his outstretched hands. It looks miserable. I jump back in bed and close my eyes.

Two days of hiding, and now I have to face it. I know the Polinski brothers will be out for me. I picture my body flopping around like a rag doll between punches, their screeching laughter ringing in my head.

I knock on Lola's door earlier than normal, hoping to avoid other kids along the walk. When she's not ready to go, I leave on my own, practically sprinting the whole way. I hide behind cars, scurry along the sides of buildings, and hurry past Jesus and his outstretched arms, staring down at me from the stained-glass window of St. Columba.

That's when I see three of the Polinski brothers huddled together just beyond the entrance, whispering secrets and sneering to each other. They are already here.

"There he is," I think I hear from their direction. My stomach drops, and the base of my head begins to throb. I rush inside, standing before a statue of Mary in the church lobby and weighing my options. She is draped in porcelain white cloth, holding her hands to her heart. There are ceramic tears on her cheeks falling into a basin of holy water. I take some and bless myself a few times.

"Watch over me, okay?" I whisper to her, as holy water drips down my forehead. I look up and can swear she looked me right in the eye.

I dart into the church pews and hide near the front, crouching down. My chest rises and falls waiting for the bell. *Thank you, Mary.*

"Hey, Jimmy."

Oh no.

"Down here."

I look under the church pew and see a set of boots and a pair of overalls crouched down, out of sight. The bell rings, and the youngest Polinski brother pops up and rushes toward class.

151

"Who are *you* hiding from?" I say, following him down the hall.

"My brothers, just like you," he replies. "Come on or we'll be late."

We slide safely into class at the last moment, and I shrink slowly into my seat, my head down.

The Polinskis are not in jail, and I'm not exactly sure if that's a good thing. Jail for the Polinskis—at least for three of them—would solve my problems. I wouldn't have to run. I wouldn't be scared all the time. I wouldn't have to pretend that they are my friends, or that they didn't steal from us all those years ago. I just wouldn't have to think about them anymore.

I glance back to the youngest Polinski brother—the same brother who didn't want to grab my ankle at the roundabout, who helped me up during Johnny-on-the-pony, and who told me to follow his lead that night at Dilworth's car. I was right—he is different.

Father Ryan is writing a quote from an old A's player, Shoeless Joe Jackson, on the blackboard. Joe was kicked out of baseball before I was born for cheating at a World Series with the White Sox, and Father Ryan has made him a common topic about sin and forgiveness during religion class. Looks like we'll be talking baseball later today.

Lunchtime comes, and I make sure that I am always near a teacher or walking closely between other kids. I'll have to add a note to Rule #19. Something like: *Never be alone when the Polinskis are out to get you.*

"Did ya hear 'bout the Polinskis?" Santa says in between bites of his bologna sandwich.

"No," I say. My voice cracks a little.

"We did!" Matty says. "Pa says they almost got caught by the cops again. He told us to stay away from them."

"Me too. Maybe they'll be expelled," Santa adds and looks at me. "You didn't hear nothin'?"

"No. I didn't," I reply, looking down. I hold my hands on my lap to hide the shaking. Nobody seems to know *exactly* what the Polinskis were doing, but the stories from the neighboring tables become increasingly more sinister:

. . . broke right into a lady's house . . .

. . . stole a car and sold it for parts . . .

. . . slashed tires up on 26th Street . . .

I turn my head quickly to see who mentioned 26th Street, and catch a few of the Polinskis glancing over at me. I quickly look away. Lunch ends, and I wrap up my uneaten meal.

Class starts again, and I choose to keep quiet and just listen, which becomes easier once Father Ryan starts his religion lesson. We've become accustomed to him creating lessons around the building of the Spite Fence, and on these days, we are all ears. Ma thinks he uses the wall to "keep all you boys engaged."

Today's lesson involves the Seven Deadly Sins, and he begins a long speech about what the wall will do to our

153

neighborhood. I listen closely. He is the only adult who will *really* talk about the wall.

He starts with greed and brings it back to Shoeless Joe Jackson.

"His whole life would have been different if he didn't give in," he says.

"But he says he's innocent," someone says behind me.

"Yes, well, we'll never know, will we? What we do know has all the earmarks of greed. They took money to throw a baseball game. The question is, will people eventually forgive him?

"Let's bring it back to 1934," he continues. "Greed tugs at us. It challenges and tests our resolve. Can we turn down something that might make us happy, if it is acquired in a malicious way? What about turning down something that affects our livelihood? Is it greedy to take something that isn't ours to feed our family or put a roof over our heads?

"And what about our neighborhood. Is that right-field wall a symbol of greed? When they build it, will we forgive them?

"Mr. Polinski." He looks over to the oldest Polinski brother. "Can you name some of the other Seven Deadly Sins?"

I can name three of them: Polinski, Polinski, and Polinski.

"Well, greed." Polinski pauses. "Lust." There is a muffled laugh throughout the room. "Wrath." Polinski immediately looks at me, and I quickly look away.

Father keeps his back to us as he writes on the chalkboard. He adds pride, gluttony, sloth, and envy. "Mr. Polinski, can you give me an example?"

"Yeah, sure. How 'bout, 'When I get my hands on that good-for-nothing traitor, he's gonna feel my wrath.'" The last word is emphasized, and he stares at me.

"That's one example, I guess." Father looks at him and crinkles his forehead. "Now, how do these sins relate to our little situation?"

We've always been taught that there are minor sins, the ones we say in confession. The *forgive me, Father, for I have sinned—I cursed four times this week, pushed my sister in the backyard, snuck out after bedtime, and buried a fish at first base* kind of sins. But the Seven Deadly Sins are the big ones, the ones we don't speak about.

Father Ryan smiles. "Take our beautiful stained-glass window. These are gray, depressing times that we are in—soup lines and fathers out of work. But that window—that window is a symbol of pride. It represents what is possible. We delight in its beauty—Jesus and his outstretched arms, welcoming our parishioners. Look closely and you see the doves, the rays of sunlight, the red heart, blue sky, and green trees. All captured in one scene. Shibe Park is the same. As a community, we have a sense of pride and beauty that the ballpark provides."

"Not everyone," I hear from someone who sounds an awful lot like a Polinski.

"But I thought pride was a deadly sin?" Matty calls

155

out. "It's right there, on the board."

"Very true! Very true. Pride is one of those words that has a negative and a positive meaning. I'm not talking about the kind of pride that is vain. No, I'm talking about the kind of pride that helps a community feel content and fulfilled."

He takes a deep breath as vacant expressions wash over all of us.

"I feel that I've lost you," he continues. "Let's have a little fun. For homework, I want everyone to write this list of sins. Then write how John Shibe and Connie Mack will benefit from doing the opposite." The class groans, and I feel a wad of paper hit me from the back. I don't look to see where it came from.

Father Ryan waits for the class to calm down and continues. "Let me explain further. The opposite of these sins will help us create our own destiny in this community. The seven virtues are ideals to live by. For example, Mr. Frances, how can we create our own destiny?"

I stare at him blankly and think.

"Okay, let's try this—what *is* the opposite of greed? What is the opposite of someone taking money?"

"Giving someone money?" I say.

"Exactly, and what's another word for giving away money?"

"Charity."

"Yes! Right, Mr. Frances. The opposite of greed is charity. And how can the owners of Shibe Park be charitable right now?"

A better question is how can the Polinskis be charitable right now.

"They can stop the plans to build the Spite Fence and let us watch the game from our rooftops. And they can start winning. Folks will buy tickets like they did in '29 if they just win a few games." The class laughs.

Father Ryan smiles. "Well, stopping the wall would definitely be charitable. The winning may be the opposite of another sin—sloth. Can anyone tell me the opposite of sloth, or neglect, or being lazy? Go ahead, call out some things."

A few words come from around the room—*diligence, patience, kindness.*

"Exactly," Father Ryan says. "For homework, think about the others. Talk with your parents. Discuss with them how destiny is created through these virtues." We hurriedly scribble down what's written on the chalkboard.

The bell rings, and Father Ryan stops us from gathering our things. "Keep this in mind. The A's may not be so guilty of the Seven Deadly Sins, but they certainly can benefit from doing the opposite. It's a good lesson for all of us."

Another wad of paper lands in my lap. I open and read the one word written.

REVENGE.

I crumple it up and decide that it's time to create my own destiny.

23

You're born with two strikes against you,
so don't take a third one on your own.
—Connie Mack

I successfully sneak out after school and run toward home. The route has slick, icy patches all over the sidewalks, and I go a longer way to avoid the Polinskis. Father Ryan and his words are running through my head.

Create your own destiny. It sounds an awful lot like a rule.

Connie Mack sure knows how to create his own destiny.

I tried to create my own destiny, and nothing has changed. Jimmie Foxx didn't argue for us. Dilworth didn't miss the meeting. But the Polinskis? I'm destined to be beaten by them. Over and over again.

I spot one Polinski brother to my left and scramble. He hasn't seen me yet, and I scurry around the front corner of the ballpark near the house. That was close. I look up at the castle-like dome that houses the offices of Connie

Mack and John Shibe, all closed up while the players are off with their families and Mack is with the all-stars in Japan. It's behind those windows where important baseball decisions are made.

I sense something in front of me when I barely hear a desperate "*KID!*" My body collides with a tall man who falls in a clump of grunts and thuds. Dark wool scratches my face, and I fall on top of him in a heap, my head hitting the concrete. I see a hat roll down the street and close my eyes.

"*Hey kid. Hey kid. HEY KID!*"

My eyes open to a man kneeling over me and yelling in my face. His pointy nose is just a few inches from my own, and he is slapping both of my cheeks. I throw my hands up to stop him.

"Cut it out!" I say. He sits with a thump on the concrete and puts his head between his knees. I sit up and wonder if I'm in a dream. I look around and see the Polinskis on the other end of the block looking at me. Not a dream. They are waiting for me. Whoever this guy is, I have to stick with him.

"You all right, Mister?" His blue wool overcoat is covered in snow, and his parted hair has gone to the wrong side, sticking almost straight up. His glasses are crooked, and his face is scratched a little. He looks around for his hat. This guy is a mess.

"I'm sorry, kid. I couldn't see with holding all of this." He motions to the ground where big tubes of white paper, stacks of binders, and some large yellow envelopes are scattered. "You all right? I need to be more careful." He starts to get up, muttering some *ouches* along the way.

"No, no, sir. It's my fault. I wasn't looking either."

"Are you certain you didn't hit your head too hard?" he asks again.

"Nah. Can I give you a hand?" I start to help him collect his things.

"That'd be great, but I have to bring these up to Mr. Shibe's office today, and I don't think you are allowed in." He's motioning to the very Shibe Park office windows that I was looking up to.

"I'm James Frances, but everyone calls me Jimmy Frank." I stick my hand out to shake his.

"Lester Pott. Nice to meet you."

"What is this stuff, anyway?" I ask, as we both gather the clutter.

"Blueprints, diagrams, order forms. You name it, it's here. They're making some changes to the grounds before next season, and I've got to deliver these for Mr. Shibe to look over. He wants everything to be ready for Mr. Mack's approval when he returns from his trip."

I stop in my tracks at the mention of blueprints and changes.

I was meant to bump into Lester Pott. Father Ryan's lesson rings in my head of the seven virtues and destiny— *hard work, commitment, dedication.* I quickly compose

160

myself, try to act casual, and clear my throat. This is *my* destiny.

"You can trust me. I'm going to be batboy next season."

"Is that so? Batboy, huh? How'd you land a job like that?"

"I'm *very* responsible."

At this point, I'm carrying just about everything under both of my arms. He motions for me to follow and fumbles in his pocket for the key as he approaches the employee entrance. I follow his lead as if I don't know where I'm going, even though I know every inch and crack in Shibe Park.

If this guy is some sort of architect or building planner, I sure could give him an earful about what needs to be fixed. Maybe another day I'll tell him that the left-field stands are shaky, the clubhouse could use better venting, the dugouts can't really hold a full team, and the brittle wooden outfield walls have already sent more than one great player to the hospital.

As we walk through the door, I'm very familiar with where we are going. I've never been inside the offices, but I still know that the stairs leading up are narrow, the third step is almost broken, and the railing starts halfway up.

Again, he fumbles with the key a bit and opens the office door, which is creaky and shorter than it seems from the outside. He motions for me to walk into John Shibe's office.

From outside of Shibe Park, these offices sit on top of the center turret, a rounded castle-looking building that has a royal feel to it. I pictured the office as being large and luxurious, fitting for the kind of place where all the important baseball decisions are made. And I'm right.

The tower office is covered with dark wooden paneling and deep brown floors. The desk sits in the middle of the room—rich-looking wood, with a red leather chair and a Tiffany lamp on the side. It's gold metal, with a fancy glass shade covered in all kinds of different colors.

There is a sofa on the left and what looks like a slightly open closet door on the right. Mr. Pott places his hat and key on the desk, and points for me to put everything down. One of the tubes of paper rolls across the desk, hitting an inkwell. The ink splashes a bit, with droplets falling on the wooden desk, right next to the key.

Another opportunity. I glance up to see he's not looking.

"I'm sorry!" I say, as I use my sleeve to wipe the ink. He never even notices as I slide the key to the edge of the desk and let it fall into my other hand. I slip it into my pocket in one motion. He spins around.

"Well, that won't do," he says and I hold my breath, the key burning a hole in my pocket.

"I, ah," I stutter.

"No worries, no worries," Mr. Pott says. "No worries."

He helps clean up the ink. His voice is jumpy, and he seems nervous, but he also seems kind of goofy, and I can't imagine him having a serious conversation with John Shibe.

"Careful with that one, it's my only copy," he says. I am holding the longest and thickest tube of paper.

"Sure, Mr. Pott." I pause. "Only copy of what, if you don't mind me asking?"

"Only copy of the blueprints for a new wall in right field. He wanted it here so fast that I didn't have time to make another."

Only copy of the blueprints. Only copy of the blueprints. The words ring in my head over and over again. *Only copy.*

"I have to go home for dinner," I say abruptly. "Nice to meet you!" I shake his hand and walk out of the room. I faintly hear him say thank you as I sprint down the steps and leave through the employee door.

I realize that halfway down the street I'm calling Lola's name loud enough for everyone to hear. I dart behind a car and look in each direction for the Polinski brothers. I see one of them before he sees me. I hop onto Mrs. Carson's porch and knock on her door.

"My dear," she says, opening the door wide, and I scoot in.

"Hi, Mrs. Carson. Just wanted to see how you were doing today?" I say, completely out of breath.

"Is that right?" she says with a smile. "And I suppose it

163

has nothing to do with those two boys across the street?"

I scramble to the window and see two of the Polinskis staring at Mrs. Carson's house. Before I know it, she is outside calling across the street.

"Hello boys. Is there something I can do for you?"

"Nah," I hear one of them yell back.

"Well then, you best be getting home for supper," she says. Her voice is old and shaky, but she stands her ground with arms crossed. She returns once the coast is clear.

"Thanks," I say, embarrassed. Somehow, Mrs. Carson knows everything about everyone.

"Go on home now." She pats my back. "Be safe."

I sprint to the house and call Lola's name. When she comes to the window, I point to the roof. She's waiting for me when I pop out of the skylight.

"Hold on," I say as I lean over, breathing heavily. "Just a sec. I met the architect," I say, practically panting. "And I was in the offices."

"You just met an architect and went to an office," she says flatly.

"*Yes!* I was in Shibe's office, and Mr. Pott let me carry his papers and tubes and folders and notebooks after we collided." I touch my head and feel a swelling bump.

Ten minutes later, I've relayed the whole story.

"Wow, that's quite a tale," she says, now sitting on the bleachers.

"I have a new plan," I say.

"In the last few minutes, you've come up with a new plan?"

"Yes." I sit next to her. "Let's take the blueprints. We can just go up there and take them. And hide them, or bury them, or maybe even burn them! Just get rid of them!"

I squirm in her silence.

"No," she finally says, looking at Shibe Park. "How hard did you hit your head? Breaking in to steal the blueprints is not just a little wrong. It's really wrong. It's even worse than stealing some gas."

I don't say anything. Listening to *her* say the plan out loud makes it sound much worse than it did in my head.

"Whatever happened with you and the Polinski boys today anyway?"

"Nothing. I don't want to talk about them," I snap. "You haven't agreed with me at all lately. Geez Lola, I'm not *always* wrong. I'm trying to do this for all of us. For our families. For the money! It's not just about watching the games!"

"And I want to help!" she exclaims. "But your plans sound more Polinski than Frances. I won't steal the blueprints. Period."

"Maybe we can just misplace the plans. You know, stall everything a bit." I look at her, pleading. "It's the only copy. It might not stop it forever, but maybe it saves next season. Maybe it gives us time to convince the newspapers to be on our side, or more players involved, or to protest with signs and megaphones. Help me figure it out instead of just saying no!"

"Okay. If we can figure out a plan that's not *so* illegal, maybe I'll help," she says. "But I won't like it. Not one bit."

"Gee, thanks," I reply. "Why even do it then, anyway?"

"Because you're my best friend." She smiles, and immediately frowns, making me laugh out loud.

"Thanks," I say. I hope she knows I really mean it. "You won't regret it, Lola. And it'll be easy."

"I might regret it, but I'll still do it. Until it becomes dangerous. Promise me?"

"I promise." We look over to Shibe Park. The outfield is dusted with small patches of snow.

"Okay then, let's talk details." She springs up. "So, you want to break into John Shibe's office, take the blueprints, and put them where?"

"We can hide them under my bed, and then put them back in a couple of weeks?"

"That's stealing," she says bluntly. "It's no different than the gas. Your sense of right and wrong is all jumbled up inside of your head."

"Alright. What if we dropped the blueprints off at Mr. Pott's office, so he thinks he never brought them to Shibe Park?"

"Stealing."

"Just take them overnight?"

"Still stealing, Jimmy. If you take those blueprints out of Shibe Park, you are stealing them." I don't like how she's shifted from *we* to *you*.

"What are your ideas?"

"I'm not the one that's been up to the office. I don't have any ideas," she says.

"Gosh Lola, you aren't even trying."

Silence.

"Fine. How about we keep the blueprints in Shibe Park—just move them somewhere. Like put them in a closet or something." At this point, I'm desperate.

"Keep going." She still isn't looking at me; her eyes are locked on Shibe. "You say there's a closet in the office?"

"Yes. In the front of the office, on the right-hand side. Just a regular closet door with no lock."

"Oh, a lock! How do we sneak into Shibe's office to begin with?"

I'm happy to hear her at least thinking about the plan. I shove my hand in my pocket and dangle the key in front of her face. In a time when nothing seems to go my way, producing the key is one of my best moments.

"Jimmy Frank! Where did you find that?"

I explain how easy it was to pick up, and how Mr. Pott never missed it.

"He used it for both the front staff door and the office door. No more going over the fence. Before you tell me how wrong it is, don't forget we've been sneaking in for years."

167

"I guess," she replies. "Having this key just feels different."

"It's exactly the same," I say. "It's just through the door instead of over the wall."

"Don't you think he'll be in trouble for losing the key?"

"He won't be in trouble. I promise. This is not a big deal."

"Jimmy, I . . ."

"Lola, once that Spite Fence goes up, this will be our only way in."

"*My* only way in, you mean," she says. "You'll be in the dugout. Unless, of course, you're caught stealing the blueprints."

"Moving the blueprints." I smile uneasily.

"When is Connie Mack due back?" she asks.

"A few weeks."

"Let me think about it. If the blueprints are just sitting on the desk until he comes home, we have time. And if we do this, we'll just move them to the closet. But promise me that this is the end, Jimmy. I promise to help you, if you promise that this is it—no more schemes. Pinky rule."

I cross my finger in front of my heart. "I promise."

We latch our pinky fingers together and say Rule #17: *A pinky promise cannot be broken.*

24

Rival pitchers will rejoice and rival batsmen will shed tears when they view Shibe Park next season.
—The Sporting News, December 20, 1934

Pop is spending more time outside of the store doing odd plumbing jobs around the city. Ma continues to pick up work, and Nina is at the store just about every day after school. She continues to look for a real job, with no luck.

I do my best to work for tips. I park cars at the Baker Bowl, where nobody cares that I don't have a license—so long as I keep my head down and stay out of trouble. Sometimes I make deliveries for the shops on 22nd Street. Rainy days are the best times to land the bigger tips. I try to put at least twenty-five cents in the cookie jar each night. Sometimes it's more, but most of the time, it's less.

I devote the next weeks to dodging the Polinski brothers and urging Lola to make our move.

"Tomorrow," she always says. She continues to write in her journal, and listens to me without too many *Jimmy, you're crazy* moments. Sometimes she reads her headlines to me:

John Shibe Nabs Teens in the Halls of Shibe Park
Lester Pott Fired for Losing Key to Ballpark
Spite Fence Goes Up Despite Neighborhood Kids

Her hesitation has put off our blueprints plan, but *The Sporting News* article on December 20 about the wall helps my cause. Now it's more than just Philadelphia news. Now the whole country knows. We make plans to sneak into Shibe Park and move the blueprints before the sun comes up the next morning.

"It's a Saturday. I start deliveries in the dark anyway. You can say you're helping me."

She finally agrees.

It's difficult to sleep, and the draft that is sweeping throughout the house doesn't help matters at all. The old furnace doesn't reach my bedroom, and the tape sealing the window cracks isn't working. It takes three of my nana's crocheted afghans and four pairs of socks before I finally drift off.

The sound of the Bingle startles me awake, and I shoot up out of the bed, nearly breaking my neck in a tangle of bed sheets and blankets. Is it five a.m. already? Coming from the outside is a strange, dull, lingering light.

I stumble to the window and pull aside the drapery, feeling the sudden need to shield my eyes. A thick blanket

170

of snow has fallen in the last few hours. The sound I hear is heavy snow resting on our Bingle string and making it ring, probably on both ends.

I open the window, fighting against some ice that has formed on the edges, and reach to the Bingle string, knocking the snow off.

"Jimmy Frank! It's three a.m.! What do you want?" I look up to see Lola's head pop out of her window.

"The snow keeps ringing the bell," I reply, careful not to wake anyone else. "Besides, we need to be up in a couple of hours anyway." I motion toward the ballpark.

Even from here, I can see Lola roll her eyes.

"We can't break in now. We'll leave footprints!" Her hands motion toward the snow with a *don't-you-see-this-stupid!* sort of face, and she crinkles her mouth. I'm certain that behind that window she is folding her arms in a huff.

But she's right. The snow is covering every inch outside. It's piled on our porch roof and is still coming down heavily. It'll be tough to sneak in.

"Tomorrow is our last chance. We *have* to figure something out," I call back and close the window.

I climb back to bed and turn to watch Bing Miller circle his bowl. *Why did I wait so long?* There were so many opportunities. So many clear nights. So many times I could have moved those blueprints. What if I missed my chance?

Sleep doesn't come for an hour.

The next morning is bright with activity on the street. I'm exhausted but can't sleep in through all the noise. Men are shoveling, or taking cigar breaks and talking in the middle of the street. Ralph and Matty are already throwing snowballs over the right-field wall. There is so much *joy* outside. How can they be so happy? The little kids are laughing, pulling each other on a sled and building a snowman.

A snowman. That's it!

I grab a pair of scratchy wool knickers and sweater—better to be warm than comfortable, as Ma always says—and head downstairs. My loud feet on the stairs draw unwanted attention.

"Hold on there, Jimmy." Ma's voice is upbeat, and I'm happy she's in a good mood.

"Morning, Ma. I'm heading out. Going to make some money shoveling."

"Very good, sweetheart. But first you must help Mrs. Carson."

"Ma, come on! That will take forever!"

"Jimmy, she is old and poor, and has nobody to help her. It's the right thing to do."

"Fine." I head to the door with less spring to my step than a few minutes earlier.

There are shovels on the porch. Pop has already taken care of our house and is in the middle of the street, knee deep in snow, smoking a cigar and laughing with some of his buddies. Mr. Sheridan and Mr. O'Connor

172

are laughing too, along with a fourth gentleman whom I don't recognize. It's funny how a little snow can bring out the neighbors and lighten the mood.

"Hey!" Lola bops out of her house, hands me a hot pancake, and picks up a shovel.

"Thanks." The cold air is more than I expect, and the pancake feels good.

"I have to shovel Mrs. Carson's place. Then we go into Shibe Park and save our neighborhood," I say matter-of-factly, as I motion for her to follow, ignoring her crooked scowl.

"Into Shibe! In broad daylight!" she says, but I continue forward, even as she flicks snow on my back with her shovel. Mrs. Carson is actually tearful when Lola and I show up.

"My two saints," she says, folding her arms to protect herself from the cold.

"It's no problem, ma'am. We're happy to be here." I look over at Lola who is still scowling. I widen my eyes in a *come-on-get-over-it* way, and she forces a smile.

"Tush now, I know you'd rather be outside playing. I didn't fall off the haystack yesterday."

"Who has ever really fallen off a haystack?" Lola wonders out loud. Mrs. Carson laughs and goes back inside, rubbing her hands for warmth.

We start, and the snow is lighter and easier to move than I imagined. We'll have this done in no time.

"Look, Jimmy. I want to help. But how do you expect

to sneak in with all this activity? Maybe this snowfall is a sign . . ."

"What sign? Remember the new rule? Rule #25: *Create your own destiny*?" I walk around so she is right in front of me. "Today's our last chance, and I've got it all figured out. We can start to build a snowman by the door and wait for the street to clear. In the daylight, we can move around easier. We'll just grab the blueprints and sneak away." My confidence is surprising, even to me.

"You mean *move* the blueprints," she says with a sharp tone.

"Yes, move them."

"What if someone sees us? It's much harder to hide in the daylight. They won't think we're a couple of nice kids from the neighborhood who went exploring. They won't just kick us out and forget about it."

"Guess you got it all figured out then, don't you?" I snap. "Were you ever going to help?" Even I'm surprised with the nasty tone of my own voice.

"Well, you two sure have done a nice job!" Mrs. Carson is back on the porch, a smile ear to ear.

Lola continues to glare at me, before breaking my gaze and focusing on Mrs. Carson.

"Just about done, Mrs. Carson. How is your backyard? Do you need anything there?" Lola walks toward her and talks in a sweet, genuine tone. I suddenly feel cold and alone.

"Oh dear, you are too kind. Let's leave the back for

now—you two look like you could use a little warming up."

I'm not quite sure if she is talking about the weather or something else.

"I have some hot tea for you, and of course I have to pay you."

"Oh, Mrs. Carson, please. We don't need anything," I say.

"Everybody needs something, dear." She motions for us to join her.

The inside of Mrs. Carson's house looks like we traveled in a time machine. Along the back wall sits a red velvet sofa that was probably fancy long ago. It's worn in all the sitting places, and there are two books where a right leg should be. The rest of the room is the same— fraying rugs, peeling wallpaper, tattered lampshades. There are crucifixes scattered on different walls, and a few faded paintings that may have been nice forty years ago. Mrs. Carson returns from the kitchen and sees me studying the room.

"This house has seen better days, Jimmy" she sighs, but quickly perks back up. "It certainly brightens up with company."

The hot cup actually hurts at first before it slowly warms my fingers. I can feel the tea go all the way down my throat. I am anxious to leave, sneak inside the ballpark, and find those blueprints.

"I can't pay you any money, of course."

"We are okay," Lola emphasizes.

"I know you are okay. But I'd like to give you something anyway. Once that Spite Fence goes up, I think I'll see less of you both."

"How's that, ma'am?" Lola asks.

"You entertain me. I watch you from time to time—sneaking into the ballpark, skulking about at night. I'm afraid that when all this changes, some of your late-night antics will change, too."

We are both staring at her now. I realize my mouth has dropped open, and I quickly shut it. Lola stands frozen.

"Mrs. Carson, we . . ."

"I'm an old lady. What else have I got to do but watch everyone else?" she laughs. "Don't worry, your secrets are safe with me. I like your spunk. I sit on my porch at night wondering if I'll see you jump over the wall. You've gotten quite good at it, you know. Now, let's see. I think I've picked out the perfect things for the two of you."

She moves toward the shelf of old books, papers, and a few journals that look just like Lola's.

"Ah, here it is." She pulls out a small photo frame, wipes the dust, and admires it for a few seconds. "I think you might like this." She hands it to Lola. "You remind me of an Allender girl." Mrs. Carson puts her hand on Lola's shoulder. "You've got such energy. Don't slip into the mold, dear. Girls—women—we can do anything.

"Those Allender girls walk around with such conviction. Why, I wouldn't be surprised if I saw a photo of you one day at the White House, with an equal rights picket sign under one arm and a journal under the other."

Mrs. Carson shows me the frame. It contains an old political cartoon, like the ones in the Opinion section of the newspaper. It is a pencil sketch of a woman holding a sign that says *for democracy*, chasing a man from the Senate holding the Constitution. The drawing is signed Allender, May 1918. I smile uneasily, feeling a little left out of the conversation, which is perfectly fine. This will not help the Spite Fence or our upcoming plan.

Lola hugs Mrs. Carson, causing them both to rock. Leaving Lola's embrace, Mrs. Carson goes back to the bookshelf and picks out a book near the top shelf. She walks over to me, smiling, and holds out the book. I take and examine it, a white cover and brown writing: *As I Lay Dying*.

"Er, thanks Mrs. Carson. I really appreciate the, um . . ."

"Oh dear, not the book! Not the book!" She opens the front cover. "This, dear—here you go."

Inside is a baseball card, but not like the ones in my shoebox under the bed. "Well, it's just a piece of cardboard," she says, with a touch of embarrassment. "But I thought you might like it. He's quite a player, and famous. Although I think a little overweight for a professional athlete."

"What?" I look closely. It's not like any card I ever saw before—a profile shot of a player in a navy hat, coat, and socks, with white pants. The bottom of the card says *RUTH, PITCHER,* with the words *International League* underneath.

"Where is this from?" I ask, turning it over and studying it a bit longer. "This is before he was with the Yankees!" I squeal.

"Oh, who knows? My son lived in Maryland. I think he had a box of stuff somewhere and left this one behind." Lola and I both stiffen up a bit at the mention of her son, knowing that he died in The Great War.

"Tush now, none of that." Mrs. Carson notices our change. "Don't expect life to be fair."

"Rule #6," I say, just loud enough for Lola to hear, and she smiles in my direction.

"Mrs. Carson, I can't take this. It's got to be worth something."

"Well, that's why it's a gift."

"No, I mean you could sell it. Raise some money for the house or food," I say. "Oh, I don't mean to, well, I just mean that you can use the money, right?"

"Nobody will buy a silly baseball card. Not in 1934. By the time it's worth something, I'll be long gone. Tuck it away, and maybe one day you can sell it yourself. Now run along. I suspect you have a scheme or two planned for today," Mrs. Carson says, collecting our cups.

We both smile and thank her again, leaving through the front door and sweeping some leftover snow along the way, making sure the job looks neat and clean.

178

"Let me see that!" Lola examines my new baseball card and places it gently into her journal for safekeeping.

"Wait, here." I rummage through my bag and pull out the fishing line, then tie it around the journal like a package.

"Good thinking." She puts them both in my bag and takes a deep breath. "The cold air feels good."

"I still can't believe she gave that to me! I can't wait to show it to Pop."

"Seems like she's been looking out for us."

"We are always going to shovel her steps."

"And we should do other things, too."

I put my hat on and try to take advantage of Lola's good mood. "Now how about a walk through Shibe?"

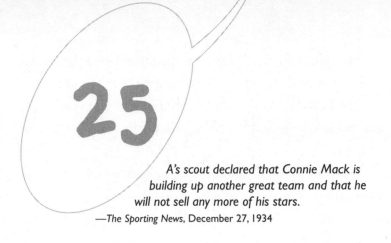

25

A's scout declared that Connie Mack is
building up another great team and that he
will not sell any more of his stars.
—The Sporting News, December 27, 1934

The sidewalk near the employee entrance to Shibe Park is busier than we expect. The streets are not clear. We set up next to the employee door and try to look busy by building a snowman, waiting for everyone to clear out, or at least look the other way.

"Keep your eye out for the Polinskis," I say, shooting looks up and down the street.

"Don't worry—they won't come around with me here," Lola says. I do believe she truly thinks she can take them on.

We did not expect the snowman itself to draw attention. All of the neighborhood kids are stopping by to lend a hand. Kids come and go, but Ralph, Matty, and Santa stay close to help finish.

"He looks naked," Santa says.

"I'll go find a hat," Ralph says, pointing to the snowman's head.

"He'll still look naked. I'll go find rocks for buttons," Santa says, walking toward Reyburn Park.

"Nobody has come in or out of Shibe for an hour," I whisper to Lola.

"Golly, my fingers are gonna fall off." Matty holds up red, uncovered hands. Ralph slaps the back of his head and calls him an idiot. They both start to walk away in search of hats and mittens.

It's the first time the street has been deserted all day. We make a dash for the door. I fumble for the key in my pocket, and my cold hands have trouble sliding it into the lock.

"Come on," Lola urges, and I shoot her an *I'm trying* look.

The door unlocks and opens easily, and we sneak in. Lola wipes away some of our footprints from outside the door just before I close it.

It's dark inside the Shibe Park hallway. I fumble in my bag and find my flashlight. We shake off our gloves and shove them in our pockets, making our way toward the stairs.

"It feels so damp and cold," Lola says through chattering teeth. I realize that I am shaking too, and I'm not sure if it's the weather or my nerves. But it's more than that. The normally warm and welcoming Shibe Park feeling is missing.

We creep along the wall, and I motion with my hand at the stairs on the right. We make it to the second floor, and

181

it's even darker than the first. The flashlight is a help, and we turn the corner to find ourselves in front of the two office doors.

I unlock the same door Mr. Pott showed me a few weeks ago. We hear a loud *creeeeeak* as the door swings open. Lola's eyebrows rise, and I grab the door before it can make any more noise. We rush in and close it behind us.

We stand flat against the door breathing heavily.

Lola motions with her chin to the desk, where there are a pile of papers and stacks of folders. No tubes, and nothing that looks like what Mr. Pott and I carried upstairs. They have to be here somewhere.

We first open the closet and spy a raincoat and some boxes of papers. I point to a safe in the corner and nudge her.

"I hope they aren't in there," I whisper.

We make our way to the desk and look through everything. There are timecards from employees, newspaper clippings of A's headlines, and letters that look like they are waiting for Shibe's signature. Yesterday's *Sporting News* article is cut out and sits in the middle of the desktop.

"This is to Fox Movietone News," I say, holding a letter from John Shibe. "He's telling them that they won't be able to gain news footage from the rooftops next season."

"And look at this! The Yankees offered $250,000 for

Pinky Higgins and Eric McNair. It's from someone named Ira Thomas."

"He's the A's scout. That's an awful lot of money."

"How can anyone have that much money in the whole wide world?"

"These are like the purchase orders at Pop's store." We continue to look through the pile. There are orders for grass seed and cleaning supplies. That's when I notice it.

The top of the invoice says Warner Central Mix & Concrete Construction Company. The materials are listed for an "Iron Wall, 20th Street side," with payment due by December 31, 1934. Lola and I stare at each other. About halfway down is a red stamp that says "Invoice," and below that in block letters: "MATERIALS DELIVERED UPON RECEIPT OF PAYMENT."

We both hear a *click* and lock eyes. *Oh no. Oh no. Oh no.*

I barely have time to think before Lola grabs my arm, shoves me around the desk and pulls me underneath, and then slides the chair in as far as it will go. We cram in the cubby hole, pressing ourselves as far back into the desk's back panel as we possibly can.

The now-familiar *creeeeeak* echoes as the door opens. We stare at each other as our eyes adjust in the small dark space under the desk. I shove the invoice into my coat pocket and quietly fumble with my flashlight to click it off.

I realize she's holding her breath, and I nudge her foot. I overexaggerate letting out some air, which prompts her to do the same. We are careful not to move an inch, careful not to make a peep. There is a shuffling of footsteps, followed by a couple of grunts.

I can't see who is in the office, but I still know. John Shibe is walking toward the desk.

Lola squeezes her eyes tight and mouths the word *no*, and I brace myself. There is sweat dripping down the sides of my temples. I wish I could peel off every layer right now. Only ten minutes ago, I was freezing from the cold.

We both silently try to squeeze back into the desk as far as possible. I pray for more space to magically appear. But there is no place to go. If Shibe walks around and tries to sit down, he will definitely find us. I'll be out as batboy. Pop's store will lose any future orders. The Sheridans will lose their uniform contract. And the Spite Fence will definitely go up.

John Shibe is now standing in front of the desk, exactly where we were only seconds before. He is inches from our heads, and we are hidden only by the back desk panel—a thin piece of wood. We can hear pages shuffle and a couple more grunts. Lola's eyes widen, and I know she's thinking about how messy we left those papers.

I hear a fizz that sounds like a bottle of pop opening, and a hard knock on the table as he sets it down.

"Dammit!" Shibe grunts, before we hear him rearrange a few more pages and let out a huge belch. Even with all of the boys in the neighborhood farting and burping all day long, I have no idea how someone can burp that loud, or sound so disgusting.

My head brushes something taped underneath the desk drawer, and a tiny piece of paper, the size of a quarter, falls on my lap. I put it in my pocket and take Lola's hands to keep them from shaking.

We continue to huddle close, tensely looking at one another. Even under this dark wooden desk, I can see that she is white as a ghost. *What have I done?*

A couple of grunts later, John Shibe shuffles his way out of the room and slams the door behind him. I wonder if he's looking for the invoice in my pocket.

Lola and I don't say a word to each other. We carefully creep out from under the desk, leave everything as it is, and move toward the door. I pause and wonder if he knows we are inside the room. Maybe he's waiting outside the door, ready to pounce. But there is really nothing else we can do. It's our only chance to escape.

I open the door and go first, see that the coast is clear, and wave for her to follow. She carefully closes the door and doesn't bother locking it. We hustle through the hall and down the steps and rush outside. Lola doesn't even check to see if the street is clear before she pulls me out. We look at each other as the door closes behind us.

"Hey! Where'd you guys come from?" A confused Santa looks up with his eyebrows raised. I smile, relieved.

"Dipping into your father's whisky again?" Lola says. Santa looks at us like we are the crazy ones, which it's obvious that we are. The snowman now has a top hat, twigs for arms, and rocks for the nose and eyes. Santa pulls a pipe from his pocket and adds it as a finishing touch. We both try to act as calm as possible.

"Doesn't he look great," I say.

"Perfect," she replies.

There are a thousand things running through my head and an invoice in my pocket.

We need to get home, and we need to get home *now*.

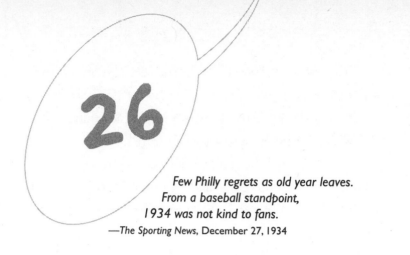

26

Few Philly regrets as old year leaves.
From a baseball standpoint,
1934 was not kind to fans.
—The Sporting News, December 27, 1934

"I'm sorry," I say. My words break an uncomfortable silence as we walk around the corner toward our houses.

"Stop apologizing to me," Lola says. "I knew what I was getting into."

"You aren't mad?" I say.

"Of course not. We made a deal, even if I didn't like it. And I can't say I told you so. But . . ." Lola smiles.

"No, you can't say that. Rule #21," I snip. "*Never say I told you so.*"

"But don't be blind, Jimmy. You know that was a little crazy."

"What's that supposed to mean?" I say.

"Nothing," she says, giving in. "I don't want to fight anymore."

"We aren't fighting. Just disagreeing. People *disagree*, Lola."

187

"Sure. And we'll laugh about this one day soon. Just not now. I'm cold and tired."

"Okay. See you later!" I say in a high voice that makes me sound like I'm trying too hard.

"Sure. See you," she replies, and walks into her house.

Dinner comes and goes, and I can barely think about anything. I slurp down spaghetti and bean soup, eager to leave the table.

"How is Mrs. Carson doing?" Ma asks.

"Fine."

"Is your friend Santa still around? When are they moving?" Pop asks.

"Don't know."

"You didn't make any money today, did you?" Nina asks.

"No."

"I thought you were gonna shovel," she digs.

"How's *your* job search?" I scoff.

"Okay, that's enough," Ma says. As the minutes tick away, I'm more and more eager to take a closer look at that invoice burning a hole in my pocket.

Pop and I finish drying the dishes while Ma is at the table drinking a cup of coffee.

"Can I go to my room?"

"Of course, dear. Thank you for helping," Ma says while listening to *Amos 'n' Andy* on the radio.

I run to my room and pull out the invoice, crumpled

in a ball, and examine it again. It is definitely a bill, and probably the only copy they had. The words "materials delivered upon receipt of payment" stand out. At the very least, if they forget to pay this bill, I'll have delayed the shipment of materials. And then maybe the season will start, and they'll have to wait to build until next year.

But where are those blueprints? They were supposed to be waiting for Connie Mack. I need to talk to Lola. Maybe this invoice will give us some time to figure out a new plan.

As I'm examining the quantity of metal sheets, green paint, cement, and hours of labor that it will take to install the wall, I remember the small piece of paper that was taped underneath the desk.

Where did that go? I search through all my pockets and find a tiny note crumpled up in a little ball in my winter coat. At first glance, it seems just like a piece of scrap paper with random numbers. But when I look closer, there are little dashes in between five sets of double-digit numbers. It looks like a combination. The combination to a safe.

I tug on the Bingle and stick my head out the window. No response. There is too much snow for the roof, so I run down the steps, burst onto the porch, lean over the rail, and knock loudly on the door. I stand there staring at the paper, tapping my foot. Where is she? Dinner should've been over a while ago. I hop over the small rail and tap again.

"Lola," I knock on the door. "*Lola!*"

She opens the door and looks at me with that sideways glance. I can see our breath in the cold, and there is an awkward silence as I try to figure out how to start.

"Here," I decide to just give her the invoice.

"You stole this!"

"Well yes, but I didn't mean to. It all happened so fast. You saw that. I was holding it and I must've shoved it in my pocket." This is not untrue, but my voice is high and squeaky as I try to explain.

"So you stole it."

"No! I also have *this*." I proudly show her the small piece of paper with the numbers on it. My feet shuffle in the cold.

"What is this?" she asks.

"I found it under the desk."

"Oh, like you *found* the invoice?"

"Yes." I choose my next words carefully. She's concentrating on all of the wrong things. "Another thing I didn't mean to take, but like I said, it all happened so fast, so quit nagging." None of this is untrue, and she seems to believe me.

"What is it?"

"Don't you see the dashes in between?" I wait for her to look more closely, but quickly lose patience. "I think it's the lock combination to the safe we saw in the closet. If we can open it, maybe we'll find those blueprints, or something even better that will stop them. We are so close, Lola, I can feel it!"

"Jimmy Frank, you stop this right now!" Lola throws both papers at my feet, and I scramble to pick them up. "We made a pinky promise! No more. All I could think about under that desk was how my parents were going to lose the only steady business they have. We can barely afford *anything* anymore! Neither can you! Just stop this—it's too dangerous!" Her face is bright red.

"I'll put the invoice back. I'll put the numbers back under the desk. But we didn't *actually* move the blueprints, so the thing I promised is not *actually* finished. I'll just take a peek into the safe. It'll be harmless."

"Do you hear yourself? All of your ideas have been *great*. Right? Just ask Jimmie Foxx or Mr. Dilworth or Mr. Pott. Now you want to break into somebody's safe? Why can't you see how you are putting all of us at risk? We'll *all* lose more than a view if you keep going!"

"Fine!" I stomp down the steps, hurt and unable to control my anger. "Fine! You'll be sorry, Lola, when you're walking around without any friends, because *I* was your only friend. Fine!"

"Why are you yelling at *me?*" she cries. "And what about the rules? Rule #2: *Things always happen for a reason*! What about Rule #10!"

"*Count your blessings?* Please! And what about Rule #12?" I yell back. "A *best friend* would stick with me!"

"This isn't burying a dead fish at first base," Lola says more softly, tears starting to stream down her face. Her bottom lip begins to tremble. "I *am* your best friend."

"You *were* my best friend," I snap.

I grab my bag and start to run.

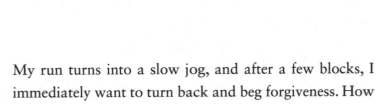

27

My run turns into a slow jog, and after a few blocks, I immediately want to turn back and beg forgiveness. How could I have said that? How will I face her?

I find myself in front of St. Columba. I sit on the stoop and bury my head in my hands, thinking about the last ten minutes. What have I done?

"Frank," I hear from the side and recognize the voice immediately. It echoes in my head as I try to find the courage to look up. I see the eldest Polinski brother standing there with his arms crossed. With all of today's events, I almost forgot all about them. It's like they've been standing here for weeks, waiting for me to be alone.

"Hey, Jimmy."

I look to my left and see the two middle brothers coming closer. The youngest one is stopped a few feet

193

behind them. I stand up, my knees shaking. I'm surrounded, and the only way out is a locked church door behind me.

Be brave. Create your own destiny. Always look people in the eye.

"Heya, guys." Boy, do I sound stupid.

"You know, Billy here got called in by the cops." The oldest Polinski is pointing to one of the other three brothers. Nobody has ever called them by their first names, so I have no idea which one he is pointing to. I sure hope it wasn't my friend.

"You don't say." I try to sound calm.

"We were able to dodge that cop your little friend sent, but Billy got pulled in the next day. They couldn't prove nothin', but you ran away like a scared little baby. We couldn't even take the stuff. You're gonna be in a world of hurt, Jimmy Frank. You're gonna have to pay."

"Oh, wow. Sorry, Billy. I didn't realize that. Look, I was all set to do it. I was being pulled away. And it wasn't Lola's fault. She didn't . . ."

"Lola!" I hear them start to laugh. "Your ugly-faced girlfriend."

"Leave her out of this."

"Oh yeah? What are you gonna do, Frank?" They start toward me, and I try to run when I feel a thump on my back and an icy stinging on my face. I can't catch myself before I fall to the ground. I look up and see another snow-ball flying through the air, hitting me squarely in the nose. I put my head down as blood drips onto the white snow.

I try to gather some snow myself and toss it in the air, but it breaks up in little pieces. The three Polinskis start to laugh. They pelt me with a constant stream of icy snowballs. I cover my neck with my hands, bury my head, and curl into a ball.

"*Stop!*" screeches through the air from my left. It's the youngest Polinski, who is pulling at the arm of one of his brothers. The brother pushes him down and tells him to scram.

Little shards of ice are breaking any uncovered skin, and freezing cold water begins to drip under the neck of my coat. Every time I try to stand up, the packed balls of snow force me to collapse to my knees.

"Jimmy!" I hear Lola's voice and look up to see her hands over her mouth.

"Saved by your girlfriend again?" A middle Polinski starts toward her. They all laugh.

"Get out of here, Lola," I spew. The words sound harsh and ungrateful. They are closing in on her, and I say anything I can to keep her safe. "Just go back home. I can handle myself."

"I got this," Lola says, loud and strong.

"GO AWAY!" I scream.

Lola stares at me before turning to the oldest brother.

I can't make out what she says to him, but it gives me just enough time to reach down and grab some snow. I roll it in between my palms, making a smooth ball of ice the size of a baseball.

The brothers start for me again, and this time the snowballs are coming faster. They are mumbling under their breath, and I hear a jumble of curse words, my name, and Lola's name in the mix.

"Take this, Jimmy Frank!"

One of the brothers winds up like a baseball pitcher, but at the last moment turns just enough to aim for Lola. The block of ice hits her squarely in the stomach, pushing her to the ground with a grunt.

"Lola!" I scream. I feel a sudden shot of energy, swing around, and hurl my own ball of ice into the air. But my feet give out from under me, and the snowball changes direction just enough to whiz past the brothers and straight toward the stained-glass church window.

I look up and see the colorful crystal Jesus—finally—looking at me square in the eye, a split second before my snowball smashes straight through the center. Shards of color rain down as glass shatters onto the ground, dotting the white blanket with shiny yellow, green, blue, and red gems.

For just a moment, I stop and stare before chaos erupts. I dash toward Lola and pull her up, and we run in the opposite direction from the Polinskis, who are making their way down 24th Street. Their cackling

196

laughter becomes fainter and fainter as we sprint, not looking back.

I hear one of them yell "GOODBYE, MR. SPALDING!" followed by another round of laughter, some angry yelling, and a duck-sounding car horn. The noise and commotion fades in the distance as we continue to run.

A few feet behind me, Lola says something that I can't make out.

"What? Keep going to the park," I yell back to her.

She doesn't reply.

"Lola?"

Silence. I turn and stop in my tracks—she is not following me.

I look down a couple of streets before slowly sneaking back toward the church, keeping in the shadows and avoiding streetlamps. There is no sign of her, until I turn the corner and see St. Columba in front of me.

I hide and watch Lola. She has taken off her hat and is gathering the pieces of glass in it. The church door opens, and Father Ryan stands at the top of the steps, hands on his hips, assessing the damage before making his way down. Lola stands there waiting.

He points his finger at her, then at the window, then back at her. Lola is staring at his shoes. I realize she's going to take the blame for me. I feel like I just got punched in the stomach again.

Why is she doing that?

I turn and run, going two blocks before it all settles in.

I can't let her do that.

By the time I make it back, there is no sign of Father Ryan or Lola. The church doors are locked. I head toward 20th Street, sure that they are heading for our houses, but again, there's no sign of them.

I wait under the porch, readying myself to come out the moment Lola shows up, but she never does. The street is still and eerily quiet.

Where have they gone?

"Come out, come out, Jimmy Frank." Three Polinskis suddenly break the silence, strolling down the street like a gang on the prowl. The sound of glass shattering on a car window breaks their chatter, and a chorus of wicked laughter follows.

"There they are!" says a deep voice from the end of the street, and more voices follow. The three Polinskis turn and run in the direction of Reyburn Park, with police officers close behind.

I peel out from under the porch and sneak in the other direction, around the front of the ballpark and onto Lehigh Avenue. Lola's got to be around here somewhere.

"This way," I hear an officer grunt, out of breath. They've changed direction, and their quick footsteps sound like they're only a few feet away. I spy the Shibe Park employee door to my right, quickly fumble for the key in my pocket, and slide in.

My back to the door, I hold my breath as the officers

run by. I look to my left and make sure the coast is clear.
I look to my right and realize that I'm all alone.

28

I wander along the closed concessions and rummage through my bag for my flashlight. When I turn it on, I see a rat scurry into hiding. That's just perfect.

The guilt weighs so heavily on my chest, and I sit on a ballpark step to catch my breath. I can taste the blood dripping from my nose. What has happened to me? How did I get here? I've betrayed my best friend in every way possible.

My thoughts jolt from one thing to another: spewing mean words at Lola, the broken church window, hiding under that desk. Then I see Pop and Ma at the store, and I picture us on the roof watching a Jimmie Foxx home run. I can't keep my head organized—it's almost too much to handle. But it all comes back to Lola. What have I done?

I find the white and red first aid station and try the

key in the lock. It works, and I gather some tissues to stuff in my nose. I relock the door behind me and walk down toward the left-field stands, wandering without a destination. That's when I spot it.

There, under the stands, is the boat I saw at the end of last season—the same day that I brought Jimmie Foxx his pie. It looks like someone is working on it. It's only halfway painted, a deep red-brown color, and there is a hatch open that looks like an engine. The name "Ethyl-Ruth IV" is painted on its side. This must be the reason those left-field lights are always on.

I make my way down, crawl in, and slink back in the cushioned driver's seat. I pull my bag off and throw it onto the passenger seat, when Lola's journal slides out. She'll never forgive me. I take the journal and hold it to my chest, close my eyes, and try to forget the events of the last few hours.

"May I sit down?"

My eyes pop open. I have no idea how much time has passed. I look up and see a tall, skinny man standing to the right of the boat. I feel a sudden panic as Connie Mack comes into focus.

I clear my throat. "Yes, sir."

Connie Mack smiles. Not an *I-got-you-now* kind of smile, more of an *amused-grandpa* kind of smile. He's holding some mail and a few newspapers and places them in the boat, then pops himself over the side and eases into the passenger seat. He acts more like one of the young players instead of a seventy-two-year-old man.

"Jimmy, right? Frances Hardware?" he says.

"Yes, sir. I'm James Frances." He looks at me like that doesn't sound right. "Jimmy Frank," I explain.

"Yes, yes. That's right. Our batboy next year, no?"

"Yes, sir."

"I've just returned home from a trip to the other side of the world, and you were the last thing I expected to find when I came down to see if Mr. Shibe had moved this yet." He taps the boat and continues, "I almost didn't recognize you. Looks like you've been roughed up a bit." He motions to his nose, and I can just imagine how my face looks.

"Yes, sir." We sit for a while, looking forward as if there is a vast ocean in front of us.

"Well then, Mr. Frances. Is there anything you want to share?"

"No, sir."

"All right, that's fair. But I have to warn you—the more you tell me, the less my mind will wander."

I look up at him, trying to figure out what he means. But I don't know what to say.

"You've broken into my ballpark and are stowed away in Mr. Shibe's latest project. There has to be a level of trust between us, especially *if* you are going to work for me next year."

"I haven't stolen anything, sir—honest."

"Yes, it looks like you were taking a nap." I look up and know that I can't hide my guilty face.

"All right then, let me escort you out," he says, disappointed.

He starts to leave when I grab his arm.

"I did do something bad tonight." My voice is shaky, and my eyes urge him to stay. It's my turn to talk.

I explain about the fight and the church window, trying to find Lola, and hiding from the Polinskis. He nods slowly as I finish, hands me a handkerchief, and motions to my forehead. I blot some blood and realize there is a cut above my eye.

"That is quite a story. And you are hiding from them here? How is it that you have a key to the side door?"

I might as well come right out and tell him everything. Father Ryan echoes in my head—*create your own destiny.*

"Mr. Mack, why are you doing it anyway? What will you get out of building a big green wall?"

Connie Mack lets out a deep breath and sits back into his seat.

"You know, you aren't the only ones upset. The news is spreading across the country. Say, how do you know the wall will be green? That hasn't been written anywhere so far," he asks in a calm tone. "And the key?"

"I—I borrowed it from Mr. Pott. It wasn't his fault. I bumped into him on the street. Then Lola and I . . ."

I stop. "Do you know Loughrea Sheridan? She's the one who took the fall for me tonight. My best friend. The tailor's daughter?"

He smiles. "Yes, I believe I do."

Ten minutes later and Connie Mack knew it all.

Foxx. Dilworth. Blueprints. Safe.

And Lola.

29

"Well, Jimmy. You certainly have been busy this winter. And frankly, in another time and another place, I might have been angrier. But you love baseball, and I can certainly understand that. Sometimes, it's nice to be reminded why I got into this in the first place." He pauses. "You know, Jimmie Foxx brought you up a few times."

"What?" I sit straight up, and my mouth drops open.

"We had a lot of time to talk in our travels. Mostly about how Babe Ruth wanted my job," he rolls his eyes. "But Jimmie told me all about your visit to the clubhouse. Tried to convince us to stop the wall. He made a good argument too—it almost worked. But Shibe? He's the money side of all of this, and he is harder to convince. You may not know this, but one of our star players rented a room with your neighbor a few years back. Al Simmons. Shibe was all ready to order the supplies for the wall until Simmons stepped in. He really went to bat for the neighborhood."

"So why aren't you on our side now?"

"I've always been on your side. I'll never forget gazing out to right field in our first World Series back in 1910 and feeling overwhelmed by the number of fans on the rooftops and balconies. It was quite a sight. But the truth is that I don't have majority control. Yet." He smirks. "I've held off the idea for about as long as I can. Between us, I'd never have it built. I love that short fence, with all of you beyond the outfield wall, sitting on the rooftops with your feet dangling over the edges. *That's* a sight Mr. Frances. That is a sight."

"That's what I mean! So, what can we do about it?"

"Nothing anymore. It was time for me to give in. I'm a business partner and a team manager. There will be other things to fight for—eventually we'll need lights for night games, alcohol for spectators, and a lot of money for player contracts. I ask for a lot, and every so often I have to give something in return. This is one of those things. And with Foxx playing catcher for us next year, he'll probably hit fewer home runs anyway. That position is tough on the body."

"Why in the world are you having Jimmie Foxx play catcher?" I say, almost forgetting who I'm talking to.

Connie Mack chuckles. "I suppose every sports writer from here to New York is asking that same question." He sighs. "Just trying to shake things up, kid. Just trying to shake things up."

"I guess I'm out as batboy next year?"

"You certainly have done some things that will put that in jeopardy. But most of this stuff is juvenile, Jimmy. It sounds to me like your friend Lola kept you from doing anything more serious. I'd say she saved you tonight."

Connie Mack climbs out of the boat and smiles down at me.

"I just want everything to be the way it was, sir," I say in almost a whisper.

"Are we still talking about the wall? Or your friend?"

"Both, I guess."

"I can't tell you what to do next, but you've got to start taking responsibility for every area of your life."

Rule #1, I think to myself.

"I appreciate your honesty, Mr. Frances," he continues. "Not everyone is honest with me, I must say. They usually just tell me what they think I want to hear. I'll let you stay here and think about what you want to do. Just promise me that once you get out of this boat, you'll head straight home. No breaking into office safes or taking blueprints. Is that clear?"

"Yes, sir."

He holds out his hand, and I place the key in his palm.

"I trust that you know how to make your way out?"

"Yes, sir."

"And Jimmy," he pauses and puts on his hat, "come see me in a couple of months. I'd like to hear how this all turned out. Remember, if we are going to work together, we need to establish a level of trust." He smiles.

"Sir?"

"I'm not giving up on you yet."

"Two months, sir," I reply. He gives me a two-finger salute and walks away.

I sit there a while longer, leaning back and staring at the underside of the left-field bleachers. After months of hopeful ideas and grand schemes, that wall is still going up. Why did it take me this long to realize that? Lola knew all along.

We'll lose the view, and my bedroom window will now look out to a big green wall. No more sitting on the rooftop, feeling the sun on my face, or watching pitchers and catchers chat on the mound. I can't fix it anymore. I wonder if I can fix anything. My hand brushes over Lola's journal in my lap. I unwind the fishing line and open it to read her last headline:

Juvenile Delinquents Get Jail Time for Stealing Blueprints

I slam the journal closed. Reading this will betray her again, and the guilt of the night returns. Suddenly baseball and the Spite Fence feel miles away. All I can think about is Lola. I can't lose her. Rule #10: *Count your blessings.*

I've got to make a new plan. I've got to make this right.

30

Bing Miller is definitely dead. I can tell by the way his glassy eyes are staring at me through the fishbowl. I stand there frozen in my room and watch him, belly up and floating in the water. I've had so many fish die throughout the years, and for the first time, I want to cry.

There is no way to bury him in the ballpark, and even worse, there's no Lola to join me. I automatically look to the Bingle—I want to run over and give it a tug, stick my head out the window, and wait for Lola. I want her face to pop out at the other end, red and frustrated that I woke her up. But my feet feel glued to the floor, and the string lies lifeless at the window.

"Jimmy?" Ma says from her room. "Is that you?"

All it takes is her voice for me to know the right thing to do at that moment. I walk down the short hall and look into my parents' room, each in their own small bed.

Ma sits up, her eyes alarmed as I come into focus. Pop is sleeping soundly.

"Ma, can I talk to you? And Pop?"

"My goodness, Jimmy!" She quickly pulls the lamp cord. The room glows with a soft yellow light, enough to highlight the bruising and dried blood on my face. I sit on her bed, looking over to Pop.

"Something bad happened tonight." My voice shakes with each word, and my lower lip quivers uncontrollably. I stop talking and try to get myself under control.

"Jimmy," Pop rubs his eyes and sits up. "You look a mess."

"I know."

"The Polinskis?" He leans over and places his hand on my knee, taking a closer look.

"Yes. But it's a lot more than that," I say, looking down.

"Whatever it is, Jimmy, be honest," Ma says.

I guess that was something I needed to hear. My lip stops shaking, and I wipe my eyes with my sleeve.

"Lola and I had a run-in with the Polinski brothers down by St. Columba. They went after Lola, and I got so mad that I threw an ice ball at them." I pause. "Only, I slipped, and it went right through the stained-glass window."

"*Oh my goodness!*" and "*Ah, nuts!*" Ma and Pop say at the same time.

"Is Lola hurt? Where is she now?" Ma says, standing quickly.

"I don't know," I reply. "Probably home. We all ran, and when I looked back, I saw her talking to Father Ryan. I think she took the blame."

"And you just left her?" she says in a sharper tone.

"Yes, but I knew it was wrong and went back, and I couldn't find her anywhere. And then I heard the Polinskis coming after me, so I hid in Shibe Park."

"Okay," Pop says, his elbows on his knees and his hands rubbing his face. "I'll go put on a pot of coffee. Sounds like this will be a long night."

"Pop?" I say, my eyes begging for some sort of reaction. He looks at me and tussles my hair.

"We taught you better than this," he says flatly, and my eyes well up again. "Is there anything else we should know?"

"I have a lot to tell you," I say, ready to confess. I unhook their robes from the back of the door, and hand them to each of them. "I'll go put on the coffee and meet you downstairs."

"And clean up your face," Ma says. I nod, close the door, and start down the hallway, pausing to listen for their reaction through the wall.

"They sure did a number on him," Pop whispers.

"We need to find Lola," Ma says. "If they hurt her . . ."

"I'll go next door and check on her."

"That beautiful church window."

"It's going to cost a fortune."

211

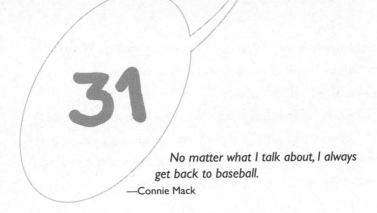

*No matter what I talk about, I always
get back to baseball.*
—Connie Mack

If you listen closely, you can hear the whispers in the
outfield. That's what Pop always says. Ghosts of players
past, asking for the ball.

I don't hear anything right now. The stadium is silent
as a photograph. I'm all alone, hopping over the fence
and walking to right field. I've got a shovel in my right
hand, and a dead fish dangling in my left.

That's when I hear the voice.

"*Jimmy*," it says softly in the distance. I swing around
and search the infield.

"*Jimmy*," it whispers again.

"JIMMY!"

I jerk awake to Ma standing over me, clean and folded
clothes in her arms. "Time to get up, dear."

"Yes, Ma." I sit up and scan the room, remembering

all the events of the night before. Bing Miller is still floating belly-up in the fishbowl, and a things-to-do list is on my bedside table. Ma places the clothes on the end of the bed, and I spring to life.

"Ooooooooouch!" I yell. Every muscle screams at my movement, and I force myself to slow down and try to stretch out the soreness. I carefully inspect fresh bruising on my arms and legs. I don't even want to look in the mirror.

Uncontrolled grunts come from my mouth as I slowly put on my clothing. I pick up the list and head down to breakfast. Pop is talking to Nina as I enter the kitchen.

"Morning," he says in a deep, sleepy voice, and turns his attention back to her. "Open the store and just sit tight until we are done."

"Okay. I got it covered." She stands up and turns to me. "Nice face. Makes you look tough."

I realize she's trying to be nice. I smile weakly, and I slowly take her seat across from Pop.

"Breakfast?" he says.

"No, thank you." I look down at my list. He studies me a bit.

"Let's go over it again," he says and takes the paper from me.

"I know it by heart," I say.

I rattle off the list in order. Of course, he doesn't

know that the first thing I have to do is bury Bing Miller for luck.

To Do
1. *Confess to Father Ryan.*
2. *Confess to the police.*
3. *Apologize to Lola.*

"A short list. That doesn't mean this is going to be easy," he says, handing it back to me and looking at his watch.

"Not easy." I take a deep breath. "Also, I forgot to show this to you yesterday." I pull the baseball card out of the journal. "Mrs. Carson gave it to me. It was her son's card. It's worth something, right?"

"This must be twenty years old." He closely examines both sides.

"I don't deserve it. Not after last night," I say. Ma and Pop exchange looks.

"It is very special," she says, looking it over. "You can learn a lot from Mrs. Carson's goodwill. Be sure to thank her properly. But right now, we have even more important things to do."

"And I don't want to hear the words baseball or Spite Fence one time today. Not once," Pop says. "We leave in thirty minutes."

Despite pain with every motion, I hurry to the

basement and reach in the back corner for the dark bag of tulip bulbs lying dormant for the winter. I collect one bulb and a small orange clay flowerpot and fill it with potting soil. I find an empty matchbox on the floor and run back to my room.

Time to bury Bing Miller. I should say something.

Something, I think to myself, and I picture Lola's scowl.

"You were named after our old right fielder, Bing Miller. Lola was there when I won you at the fair." I pause as I hear Nina walking down the hall. I whisper the rest. "See, there are these boys. And there is this church window. But mostly, there's Lola. Please bring me luck. Amen."

I carefully place the fish into the cardboard matchbox and slide it closed, dig a small hole, and place the tiny fish coffin on the bottom of the flowerpot. I add the tulip bulb and top it off with rich soil. I'll have to fix Rule #13 to include burying fish in flowerpots.

"Put it on the roof," Ma says. I look back and see her leaning in the doorway, arms crossed. "The cold will keep the flower from waking up too early."

I push the skylight up and slide the flowerpot onto the roof. A little snow falls inside, and I use my towel to clean it up before it melts. I look at the wall clock. It's time to go.

"I'm ready!" I yell from the front door.

"You know what you have to do, son."

"Yes, Pop. I know," I say. He stands before me, waiting for more.

"Confess to Father Ryan. Confess to the police. Apologize to Lola." My stomach flips a couple of times.

"Confess and apologize," Pop says.

"Confess and apologize," Ma says, putting on her coat. She kisses me on my forehead and takes Pop's hand.

"Confess and apologize," I repeat. "Let's go."

32

"And where is Loughrea Sheridan now?" Officer Sherman asks.

"Home," Pop says, clearing his throat.

"Yes. I walked her home last night, after the window shattered," Father Ryan adds. "I planned to report it all this morning but was held up when the Frances family showed up at my doorstep. So, we came together."

The four of us sit around a small wooden desk in the front room of the police station. Officer Sherman has a pot belly and a uniform with bulging buttons up to his neck. His police hat and badge are on the desk, sitting on top of a stack of cut-out newspaper articles. The one on top is a headline about the rioting at the Eastern State Penitentiary last year.

There is a framed photo of him and some other officers and horses, holding a trophy, and another of him out of uniform, dressed in suspenders and a fat tie, with his arm around a lady. Ma sees me studying his desk.

"See? He's just a regular person," she whispers in my ear. "Take a deep breath."

I nod.

"We saw the church window. That was just one of many broken windows last night." The officer motions to the back room.

"What's back there?" Pop asks, and I straighten up a bit.

"The Polinski boys. They broke three car windows and slashed two tires, shattered the streetlamp over on 22nd, and broke into Kilroy's Tap Room. And that's only what we know so far."

"Now why would they do all that?" Pop asks out loud, but to nobody in particular.

"They've been pushing our limits for a while. I usually go soft when their Pa's in jail, but he's out now, so no more free passes. Waitin' for him now. Don't expect him to rush over, dirty bootlegger."

"Maybe their recklessness is a cry for help?" Father Ryan says. None of the adults nods in agreement. Neither do I.

"We found them over on 24th Street trying to pick the lock of the library. The *library*, of all places. I guess they was lookin' for a warm place to hide." He shakes his head, and looks to Father Ryan. "Okay, so take me through it."

I look at the doorway to the back room and feel panicked that the Polinski brothers are only a few feet away. When I do, I notice the trophy from the photo behind Officer Sherman on a table; it reads *Best Mounted Policeman*. Next to it is a 1929 A's World Series program, tilted up on display, and on the wall above that is a framed certificate from the Police School on Criminal Law. Something about all of this puts me at ease.

"I was asleep when I heard the window," Father Ryan explains. "Miss Sheridan was outside, picking up the glass. She told me the Polinski boys beat up Jimmy, and the window broke during the fight." He looks at me. "She didn't say it was you who broke it. And she didn't mention that she was hit in the stomach."

"She's too tough and proud to tell you she was hit," I reply.

"Has anyone talked to her parents?" the officer asks.

"Yes," both Father Ryan and Pop say. "She's at home and just shaken up. She needs some time," Pop adds.

"Okay," the officer says, scribbling something in his book.

"That's when I broke the window," I interject. "It was when she got hit in the stomach. I went to throw an ice ball at them but slipped. It went straight through. It's all my fault, and I can take the blame."

The officer sits back and studies me a bit and then turns to Father Ryan.

"Is that what you think, too?" he asks.

"What do I think?" Father Ryan asks himself. He rests his forehead on his hands. "What do I think?"

We wait while he gathers his thoughts, and I start to wonder if we'll be here all day.

"I think Mr. Frances is being honest. I think he is admirable for coming forward this morning. And in the end, I don't think it was his fault."

That's when he stands up and starts pacing the room, just like in one of his lectures.

"But he left the scene. And for all he knew, Lola was taking the blame," he adds.

But I went back! I think to myself.

"Although if I were twelve years old, maybe I would have run, too."

But I looked for her! I think to myself.

"Mr. Frances. Remember that lesson on the Seven Deadly Sins?"

"Yes, sir," I say, clearing my throat.

"And how about the opposite?"

"The Seven Heavenly Virtues?" I reply. *Do we have to do this now?*

"Exactly. I'm thinking of Temperance," he says. "It means to have appropriate actions, or in your case, reactions. At least that's one meaning. What do you think?"

"Well, I've talked to my parents. I'm on my way to see Lola. I'd like to figure out a way to pay for the window. I hope that's a good reaction? Even if it's a little late."

"A proper gesture, indeed. Officer Sherman?" Father

Ryan asks, looking to the police officer, who in turn looks at me.

"Jimmy, I think we can come to an understanding if you pay for the window. And I'm not going to charge you for leaving the scene."

"Thanks!" I say. Pop pats my back.

"But do you have any idea just how much that might cost?"

"I need to check on that," Father Ryan interjects. "I'd guess about a thousand."

"*Dollars?*" I accidentally say out loud.

"Jimmy, hush," Ma says.

"We'll figure it out," Father Ryan says, looking at all of us.

"Well that settles it then," the police officer says. "I don't mean to throw you out, but I have the Polinskis." He rubs his temples. "I think it's going to be a long day."

"Officer Sherman?" I say. "Are all the Polinksis back there?"

"Why?"

"Because it wasn't all four of them last night. The youngest one didn't hurt us."

"You mean Tommy," Father Ryan says. "I found him sleeping on a church pew this morning. I don't know how he got there, but I'm glad he found a safe place away from his brothers."

"He was trying to help us. Will he be okay?" I ask.

"The Rosato family said they'll take him in for a few

days until all of this is straightened out."

"Thank you, Officer Sherman." I stand up and shake his hand.

"Keep me posted about that window."

"Yes, sir." Ma and Pop shake the officer's hand as well, and we leave the station, heading for the church.

"A thousand dollars?" I whisper to Ma. "I'm never gonna be able to pay for that."

"Oh Jimmy, you are white as a ghost!" she says, but I can tell she's worried too. She puts her arm around me and whispers, "I'm so proud to be your mother. It sure is a lot of money, but we'll work it out. Father Ryan will not let us go hungry over some colorful glass. I promise you."

"Right," I reply uneasily. She squeezes my shoulder for a hug, and I jump in pain.

We walk to St. Columba and stand under the broken window. Father Ryan and Pop carefully break out the remaining glass while Ma and I pick up the pieces. They find a tarp in the church basement and fasten it to cover the opening.

"I'll find a few jobs and give you the money as it comes in," I say.

"Going to take more than a few jobs, Jimmy," Pop says and turns to Father Ryan. "Is it really one thousand dollars?"

"It was a beauty," he replies. "One of a kind."

"It certainly was," Pop agrees. "Look, if I lose the store, we'll have no way to pay you."

"And if we lose the house, we'll have no place to live," Ma interjects.

"One thousand dollars is impossible," I say.

"I know what's important, Mr. Frances." Father pats Pop on the back. "Let's see how this tarp works for now. Let the events of last evening settle in."

"I'll board this up tomorrow," Pop says. "Fletch will help."

"Yes, it will all work out. Maybe even better than before." Father Ryan shakes his hand.

"I'm not sure about that," I say. Father puts his hands on my shoulders.

"Son, the strength of a community is surprising. I have a good feeling about this."

"Rule #2," Ma says. "*Things always happen for a reason.*"

"But a *thousand* reasons?" I blurt out.

"Maybe," Father Ryan says. "Maybe it happened for a thousand reasons."

33

You can't win them all.
—Connie Mack

Three times. It takes me three rings of the Bingle to know that she's not answering. Maybe she isn't home.

"Drop this off for Mrs. Carson." Ma comes into my room and hands me a brown bag.

"Okay," I say.

I walk slowly past Lola's house, trying to sneak a glance in the window, but all the curtains are drawn.

"Jimmy!" I turn to see Santa, Matty, and Ralph running up behind me.

"Holy Cow!" Santa says. "You look terrible!"

"I know," I reply. "The Polinskis are at the station. I think I'm safe at the moment."

"We heard all about it," Matty says. "Geez, Jimmy. You sure took a beating."

"Everyone is talking about it," Ralph adds.

"That's just great," I say. "Hey, I gotta drop this off for Mrs. Carson."

"Come to the park when you're done," Santa says, already heading toward the alley.

"Maybe," I say. But I only want to see Lola. I walk down the street, keeping my head low and avoiding anyone's eye contact.

"You are so bruised, my dear!" Mrs. Carson says when I knock on her door.

"I was worse this morning. Ma wanted you to have this."

"Thank you, thank you. You know, Lola stopped by," she says, keeping an eye on my reaction.

"Really? What did she say? She's so mad at me!"

"She needs some time, Jimmy. That's all." She smiles softly.

"*Time heals all wounds*," I reply. Rule #8.

"While I have you here, there's something I'd like you to have."

"Yes, ma'am," I say and cross my fingers, hopeful for another baseball card. She slowly makes her way to the bookshelf and picks out a leather-bound book.

"What's this?" I ask when she hands it to me.

"It's a journal. An old one, but empty," she says. "I thought giving it to Lola might be a nice gesture. Better coming from you than from me. She told me that you had her journal and she didn't have anything to write in."

"I do have her journal. But it has blood stains all over it."

"Oh dear," Mrs. Carson says. "Well then, all the more reason for a new one."

. . .

I stand on the porch for at least ten minutes before I have the nerve to knock.

"Jimmy!" Mrs. Sheridan says, opening the screen door and stepping outside. "You look terrible!"

"Yes," I say. Hearing about my bruised face is becoming tiresome. "Can I please see Lola?"

"I'm sorry, Jimmy. Lola isn't up for it today, and she'll be helping at the store a bit more now."

"Oh." My lip starts to shake uncontrollably.

"Maybe come by in a few days and see if she's free," Mrs. Sheridan says.

"Really?" The tears are now flowing, and I wipe my nose on my sleeve. She hands me a handkerchief from her housecoat pocket. "Maybe I can just see her for a minute?" I blubber.

"Jimmy," she begins to whisper. "Lola doesn't have many other close friends. Most girls don't understand her the way you do. I think she just needs time. Don't give up on her."

"I'd never give up on her," I say softly. "I mean, I did give up on her, but I made a big mistake. Can't I just see her?"

"Not today," she replies and slips back inside.

226

"Mrs. Sheridan? Can you give her this?" I hand her the blood-stained journal.

"Of course," she says, and closes the door.

I leave her porch and sneak to my room, close the door, and sit on my bed. Will she ever forgive me? What can I do? The empty fishbowl sits on the bedside table, and I wonder if there is any real luck in the world.

Create your own destiny rings in my head. *Create your own destiny*.

I open the new leather journal and title the first entry: *Dear Lola*.

34

Foxx, who'll catch for 'good of club,'
asserts hitting will suffer as catcher. A's star
places his own choice secondary to Mack's
wishes in giving up first base job.
—The Sporting News, February 7, 1935

The snow from last December never really melted, and the winter of 1935 is one of the coldest I can remember. I lie on my bed covered in afghans, thinking about all of the things I'll be doing on this cold February day.

I stare at the empty glass bowl on the table. Maybe it's time for a new fish. I can sure use the help. *No, no, no. Create your own destiny, Jimmy.*

My weekend mornings have become very busy, and I wake up before everyone. First on the agenda are deliveries for two of the stores on 22nd Street. It's dark when I leave the house, with a dull haze filling the streets from the rising sun. I bundle up and deliver bread to Doc Hoffman's, Elrae's, and The Hop Inn, and some meats to Kilroy's Tap Room and Nick's, where the manager gives me some hot coffee. I think they are starting to forget that I'm just a kid.

My next stop is the druggist, who has me make twelve deliveries to some of the elderly and sick folks in the neighborhoods. I let him pay me, but I refuse all of the tips. No matter how much money I am trying to raise, I can't bring myself to take money from the sick. I do accept warm muffins, if they offer.

I then make my way to the library on 24th Street and help stock books. They can't pay me, but they give me an early lunch every Saturday, and that's one less meal Ma has to make.

Down every alley and on every street corner, I look for Lola. I often see her through the store window, or coming out of Mrs. Carson's house. Sometimes I wave, and she is starting to smile more and more. My insides skip every time she does. I hope one of these times she'll motion for me to join her.

But that hasn't happened yet. She still hasn't answered the Bingle, and we haven't walked to school together since that night.

At noon, I rush over to the movie theater and put on my apron and hat to take tickets. In the last six weeks, attendance is up, and the movie house manager says that's good for the economy. I just think people want to escape from their troubles and are willing to pay a dime to do so.

When it's all done, I'll probably make about twelve dollars today, and that's before whatever odd jobs I can cook up in the evening. Everyone in town knows that I'm trying to pay for the window.

Today's movie matinee is *Death on the Diamond* with Robert Young and Madge Evans. It's a whodunit that I've been able to watch in between selling tickets and pop. But I haven't seen the ending, so I make my way over to the doors to have a peek.

"Anything good, kid?" I hear from behind me. I quickly scramble from the door back to the booth.

"Yes, sir. Next show is at three p.m. Would you like a ticket?" I say, before even looking up at the person in front of me.

"Well, look at you," says Jimmie Foxx, in that same nice drawl that I heard in the clubhouse last September. A slow realization comes over his face. "I thought the next time I saw you, you'd be in an A's uniform instead of that getup. You trading baseball for Hollywood?"

"No, sir. Wow, you remember me?"

"How could I forget? I had lots of discussions with Connie on our way to Japan."

"Say, why are you here in Philly?" I ask. "Don't you have some sort of baseball academy in Florida to run? I read about it in the paper."

"Sure do. I'm heading down later next week. Takin' my tonsils out tomorrow and the Doc is up here. Ain't never been the same since Canada."

"That guy sure did bean you in the head, didn't he?"

"Sure did." He pauses and adds, "Now don't you go on telling anyone. I don't want to read about it in the evening *Bulletin*."

"My lips are sealed," I say, pretending to button them closed. The matinee has ended, and some of the moviegoers are pointing at Jimmie Foxx and whispering.

"Sorry about that wall, kid. I talked to Connie, but it was all for naught. Looks like we'll both lose out when it goes up."

"Yes, sir. I talked to Mr. Mack as well. Thank you for trying. Anyway, there is nothing we can do about it anymore," I say. "That's Rule #6."

"Ah yes, the rules. What's this one?" he asks.

"Rule #6: *Don't expect life to be fair.*"

"You got that right, kid." He leans toward me and whispers, "If life were fair, I'd still be at first base." He pulls out his money to pay. "I guess I'll see you over at Shibe."

"Maybe. To be honest, sir, I'm working to pay for a church window that I broke, mend a friendship that I destroyed, and save my job as batboy," I say.

"Save your job as batboy?"

"Yes. If I pay for the church window, I think I have a shot. But it will take forever, so we'll see. It's a long story, and your movie is about to start. I do hope to see you, so fingers crossed," I reply and hold up my crossed fingers. I always say the dumbest things around him.

"Committing yourself to constant improvement," he says, smiling.

"Hey, that's a rule, too! Rule #5!"

"Like I said before, I sure do like your rules. I guess

we are both tryin' to make the best out of what we have," he says.

I beam at the comparison.

He continues, "You do what you have to do, Jimmy Frank. And I'll see you for the start of the season."

"Hopefully, Mr. Foxx," I reply. I take his money and show him inside.

I return for the rest of my shift, and during the down times, I take out the journal from Mrs. Carson. With Lola not speaking to me, I've taken to writing in it each day to tell her what's been happening. The diary reads like a long apology letter, dotted with mishaps and funny things that I don't want to forget to tell her.

I write about parking cars during the Penn rugby matches, about learning to fix the pipes with Pop and him sending me on real handyman jobs, and about cleaning up Reyburn Park for a fancy wedding and landing a five-dollar tip.

Every night, I ring the Bingle, and when she doesn't show on the roof, I leave the journal on her side. Every morning I pick it up. I have no idea if she ever reads it. I title today's entry: *Jimmy and Jimmie Meet Again.*

35

Mack shuffles infield talent and comes up with a full hand. There are no unsigned players in the house of Mack.
—The Sporting News, March 7, 1935

The sunlight warms my face, and I spring out of bed with a shot of energy. I look at the clock: 8:01 a.m. I rush to the window to see bright blue skies and folks walking without overcoats or scarves. It's March, and spring has arrived early.

I quickly put on my freshly pressed knickers, and crisp shirt and cap, and hustle downstairs.

"Ma! Pop! MA! POP!" I stomp down each step.

"Quiet down! What's so important?" Nina asks. I walk so close to her that she can't move in any direction, and wrap my arms around her for a hug.

"What is your problem?" she says, squirming out of the way and smoothing down her skirt.

"Just wish you could come today," I say, flashing a devious smile and wrapping my arms around her again.

She pushes me lightly and actually laughs a little, before grabbing my hat and throwing it across the room.

"Me too." She tussles my hair on her way out the door. "Michele is waiting for me," she says, halfway down the porch steps.

"Have a great morning, sweetheart," Ma says through the screen door. Nina has been working for the owner of Lee's Bakery for a month now, and getting more and more hours each week. She's hoping to work full time over the summer.

I put my cap back on and walk into the kitchen. Pop is at the breakfast table reading the *Inquirer* while Ma puts a few hotcakes on a plate for me. She pats the chair for me to sit and hums to Guy Lombardo singing on the radio: *My heart's humming. Better times are coming. Have a little faith in me.*

I stare at the food, and my stomach jumps at the lyrics. "Don't you think we should be going?"

"Settle down, Jimmy," Ma says. "We have an hour until the unveiling."

"It's not just the unveiling," I say, thinking about how my job as batboy still hangs in the balance. *In the distance there's a silver lining*—the lyrics drift in from the radio, and my stomach rolls again.

Forty-five minutes later, we walk out the door, cross the street, and head toward St. Columba. I'm so proud that Ma and Pop are coming with me today. I notice that Ma is looking particularly nice.

"New hat, Ma?"

"New to me," she says in an upbeat voice, touching the edge to move it slightly. Even thrift-store clothes can make her feel good today.

We arrive at St. Columba to a small crowd. The stained-glass window is still covered with the tarp. Two ropes hang on either side, ready for the unveiling. Father Ryan is talking to Connie Mack. He motions for us to join him. We carefully weave our way through the people who are chatting and enjoying fresh tea and hot coffee. I wave to Ralph, Matty, and Santa, who are sitting on a stoop across the street.

Father Ryan is in the middle of a conversation about serving alcohol in the ballpark.

"So, the courts actually sided against you," Father Ryan says. "I didn't think it was possible. Too bad the housing commission doesn't take advice from the city treasurer."

Even on a day like today, baseball comes first. After an uncomfortable pause, Connie Mack turns his attention to us.

"Mrs. Frances, it's very nice to see you again," Connie Mack says, greeting Ma. He shakes all of our hands.

"I thought you'd be in Florida for spring training?" Pop asks.

"And miss this? Never! I had some contracts to attend to anyway, but that's now all squared away. I'm leaving tomorrow."

"Well thank you, Mr. Mack. For coming today. For all of this," she waves her hand toward the church.

"Thank me? I'm not the one who raised all the money. You should be proud of your son, Mrs. Frances. Raising $207 dollars in this economy is not an easy task." He turns to me. "You've been a busy young man. Quite the entrepreneur."

"Yes, sir. But I'd never have gotten the rest without you," I reply.

"Yes, you would have. And there is no shame in taking my help," he says.

Ma whispers in my ear: "Rule #7: *Always accept an outstretched hand.*"

"No, donating the rest was selfish on my part. People think I'm a cheap-skate, but I do like to give back. And your friend Jimmie Foxx thought it would be a good idea as well."

"Is that so?" Father Ryan says eagerly. "Is he interested in joining St. Columba?"

"Not exactly," Connie Mack says. "Foxx bumped into Jimmy this winter and started rambling on about some rules, and how I need to find ways to make amends with the neighborhood. This is a small step in the right direction."

"You still have time to change your mind about that wall," Pop jumps in, but his tone is not bitter or unfriendly. Connie Mack smiles, and they both know that the wall is still going up. There is no reason to argue.

"I left something back at the office. Will the three of you join me after we are finished here?" Connie Mack asks, and we agree. I raise my eyebrows enough for Ma to see. This is it. Batboy. I look around, hoping to see Lola in the crowd.

"She's not here," a voice behind me says. I turn to see Mrs. Carson.

"Yes, ma'am," I say. I know that Lola has been spending time with her. "I've been meaning to thank you again for the journal. I promise I'll give it to her soon, but first I've been filling it with things I want to tell Lola."

"I know. She shares it with me," she says, and I brighten at the thought of Lola actually reading it each night. *Is* she ever going to forgive me? I want to ask, but before I have the chance, Mrs. Carson says, "It looks like we are getting started."

We turn toward Father Ryan, who is trying to quiet the crowd. He motions for me and Pop, and we each take a rope.

"Thank you for coming today. Is everyone ready?" The crowd nods their heads and buzzes in anticipation. "Okay! Ready—one, two, three!"

We pull and let the tarp fall to the church steps, revealing the brand new stained-glass window to a chorus of gasps and applause.

It is even better than before—a kaleidoscope using every color of the rainbow, patterned in a way that makes each angle look different. There are yellow and green leaf crystals surrounding red roses along the edge, next to deep orange arches scalloping the circle. Blue and purple streaks jet toward the center, highlighting a golden cross over a large red sacred heart.

"This window represents the heart of this community," Father Ryan opens his remarks. "I wanted to capture that. It's beautiful, no?" he asks the crowd. Everyone nods in agreement.

Ten minutes later, after a couple of prayers and many thanks to various people in the crowd, he looks in our direction. He talks about charity and commends Connie Mack for coming through for the neighborhood—*in this respect*, he adds quickly.

Charity, the opposite of Greed, I think.

He then makes some remarks about praying for a winning season before turning the focus to me.

"Earlier this school year, we had a lesson on the Seven Virtues," he starts. "We discussed using them to create our own destiny . . ."

This part of the speech is probably only a minute or two, but it seems to take hours. I don't like the attention, and look down as he mentions something about overcoming adversity, taking responsibility, and making him proud.

The only interesting part is when he mentions that the "other parties involved" are learning their lessons in other ways, and I think about how the three Polinski brothers are spending their winter in juvenile detention.

Ma squeezes my shoulders, which I quickly shrug off. I am sure that my face is a deep shade of red.

"You've stepped up to the plate, Jimmy, and you've hit a home run."

I don't think anyone is surprised that Father Ryan ends with a baseball reference.

36

There will be no beer sold at Shibe Park in Philadelphia this season.
—The Sporting News, March 14, 1935

It takes us longer to leave than expected, with everyone wanting to shake my hand to offer congratulations, and shake Connie Mack's hand to say thank you. I finally escape to across the street and wait on the stoop with the other boys. Matty, Ralph, and Santa all came to watch. And Tommy Polinski.

Everything changed for Tommy the night of the fight. He moved in with an aunt and started coming around more and more. Ma's even invited him for dinner a few times. We haven't talked about his brothers at all, or that he chose me over them that night. I did write about it in the journal for Lola to read.

"Neat window, right?" I ask.

"I guess," Matty shrugs. "But I liked trying to catch Jesus looking at me." Ralph pushes him and knocks him off the step.

240

"That was just an old rumor," Santa says.

"I never did catch his eye," Ralph adds.

"I did. Just before my snowball went straight through the window," I say, and they all laugh, even Tommy. I join in, although I secretly wonder if he did bring me luck. Or at least guide me to create my own destiny.

"Besides," I continue, "that statue of Mary brought me luck. She helped me hide from your brothers that one morning." I look over to Tommy.

"Really?" Matty perks up.

"Sure. Just dip your fingers into the holy water, bless yourself, and ask her."

"I'll have to try that when they get out of jail," Tommy says. We all laugh nervously. I do wonder what'll happen to him when their juvenile detention finally ends.

"We'll have your back," Santa says.

"Yeah?" Tommy sits up a little straighter.

"You bet," Ralph adds. We are not a gang of fighters, but Tommy doesn't seem to care. He smiles like it's the best thing he has ever heard.

"*Jimmy*," Ma calls from the crowd.

"Time to go." I take a deep breath. "Gonna find out about batboy." They all stand and pat me on my back as I leave.

The walk to Shibe Park is quick. Ma and I let Pop and Connie Mack walk ahead of us. We hear small parts of their conversation. It sounds an awful lot like Pop is questioning all of his managerial moves, and Mr. Mack is smiling politely, letting him talk.

We enter the Shibe Park employee entrance, climb the same steps to the offices, and enter the door next to John Shibe's office. We are standing in an office almost identical to the one that Lola and I broke into, except the closet, sofa, and windows are on the opposite side. The curtains are parted, and the room is quite bright, much lighter than I remember it. There is a statue of a large white elephant on his desk.

He motions for me to sit across from him and leans back in his red leather chair. He has a pleasant look on his face, the same expression he had when we talked in the boat. Not the monster I created in my head. Not the one who is building a wall just for spite.

Here it goes. Remember Rule #3: *Say "please" and "thank you."*

"Mr. Mack, I want to *thank you* for helping me out. I'm not sure what I would've done if you didn't see me in that boat. And I'd like you to *please* still consider me for batboy."

"I never told you what to do, Mr. Frances," Mack says.

"Well, my head was just all over the place. So, thanks."

"You're welcome," he says, and I feel relieved that that part of the conversation is over. "How is your friend doing?"

I didn't expect him to ask about Lola. There is a long awkward pause.

242

"Well," I clear my throat. "I apologized right away. I mean I've tried to apologize. Like a million times." I didn't rehearse this part, and my words tumble out faster. "Sometimes I leave a Valomilk or a soda pop for her, but I stopped doing that so I could save more for the window." I pause and catch my breath.

"But we haven't talked. We even got Monopoly for Christmas and I haven't played it yet. I'm waiting to play with her."

"I bought that from Gimbels myself," he says. "For my grandkids. Fascinating game."

"I'll keep trying." I bite my bottom lip to keep it from quivering. "Every day, I ring our bell, and knock on her door, and I try to time things *just right* to bump into her. I just want to be her friend again. That's all that really matters."

Mr. Mack stands up, buttons his coat, and shakes my hand. "Time is a funny thing, Jimmy." He walks toward the closet and opens it. I see the safe in the corner and look over to Ma, catching her eye. She shrugs her shoulders.

"I forgot to bring this to the church," he says, as he hands me a brown paper bag. I stare at him blankly.

"Go on. Take a look. Try it on." I rip the bag open and see the soft white fabric. The A's elephant is staring back at me. "Everyone here needs a uniform," he says.

"Thanks, Mr. Mack! I won't let you down." I shake his hand, and it suddenly feels like spite fences and broken

243

windows are a million miles away. I have my very own A's uniform. I'm finally part of the team. I slide in each arm right over my dress shirt and begin to button, when I notice a small *LS* stitched inside near the top buttonhole, just big enough for me to see. Lola stitched this top. The little hairs on the back of my neck stand up, and I can't control my smile as I grin from ear to ear.

"I bet he never takes it off," Ma says to Connie Mack. She's probably right. I will never take this off.

"It's well deserved," he replies, and turns again to me. "I believe in you, Jimmy. And I wasn't kidding back at the church. Raising $207 is an incredible accomplishment. I see great things in your future." He walks us down the steps and to the street. The warm sun hits me and I take a deep breath. Things are looking up.

"The team will be coming back from spring training in about five weeks for the City Series against the Phillies." Pop sees the opening and starts talking about the A's most recent headlines. He jumps from Mickey Cochrane managing the Tigers, to the McNair and Higgins contracts, to Jimmie Foxx's brother playing in spring training.

"There sure is a lot going on," Pop says, scratching his chin as if he is contemplating it all. Connie Mack looks back to me, amused.

"Some of the Clubhouse Boys have already started cleaning up the grounds. Why don't you come by next

Saturday to help out? Once the season starts, you'll be our new batboy. Jimmie Foxx certainly is a fan. And I think you've earned it. How does that sound?"

"How does that *sound*?" I grin. "It sounds like I'll have the best seat in the house."

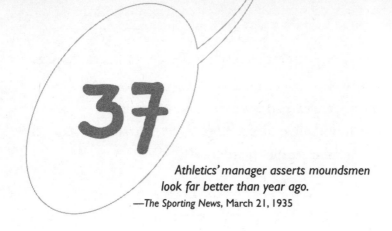

*Athletics' manager asserts moundsmen
look far better than year ago.*
—*The Sporting News*, March 21, 1935

I wake to a loud motor and a *tut-tut-tut* that shakes the entire house. I rush to the window and see my biggest fear come true. Or what used to be my biggest fear.

The Warner construction trucks have come down 20th Street and are unloading large sheets of metal and monster-size posts. Men with hard hats, overalls, and tool belts are filing out of the trucks, using gloves to handle the materials.

I try to move, but my feet are stuck to the ground. I wobble a bit and steady myself on the windowsill. It's a warm Saturday for March, and I open the window and stick my head out. The entire neighborhood has come out to watch.

I pull at the Bingle a few times—like I have done almost every day since that dreadful night—throw on some clothes, and grab the journal. I find a ribbon that Ma gave me and wrap it up.

The sun hits my eyes as I emerge from the skylight, and I squint down the row of houses. The rooftops are filled with solemn faces and people crying. Boys who are normally terrorizing their sisters or making fart jokes are sitting quietly on their benches.

Ma and Pop are at the store, and our rooftop bleachers are empty. I make my way to the lowest bench, where I sit and watch.

A moment later, I look up to see Lola standing above me. The sun, which is directly behind her, outlines her hair, and I can't tell if she is smiling or frowning. By the time my eyes adjust, she has already looked away toward Shibe Park.

She sits, lifts her knees to her chest, and hugs them. I lean back with my elbows on the bench behind me.

Even without speaking, I am convinced that Lola is back by my side. Back to our friendship. Back with me for good.

"So, I think the A's are going to be a good team this year," I say, fumbling over my words a bit.

"Oh, yeah? Your own expert opinion?" she says. I've never been so happy to hear Lola's sarcasm, and I can't help but grin.

"Not mine. Everyone's." I pull out Wednesday's *Sporting News* from my army bag, and read aloud:

Ft. Myers, Fla.—So well pleased is Connie Mack with his pitchers and Jimmie Foxx's brilliance and power behind the bat that he has come out openly and predicted that the Athletics would resume their role of pennant contender this year. "It's the best team I have had in several years," Mack said, "and we must be considered strictly in the race . . .

"I wasn't fooling. I figured the catching department to be the weak spot on our club and Foxx was the only man at my command who could change it into . . ."

"At my command," Lola interrupts.

"Sorry?" I stop.

"Connie Mack said *at my command*. He's just so powerful," she says, motioning to the construction.

"It's just a wall," I say. Lola closes her eyes and takes a deep breath. We both continue to look straight ahead and watch. "I even made a rule about it," I add.

"What's that?" she asks.

I hand her our list of rules, and she reads it out loud.

"Rule #26: *Walls don't block us from the things that really matter.*"

I smile nervously and wait for her reaction.

"That's a statement. It's not a rule," she says. I look up and begin to defend it, only to see her grinning from ear to ear.

"Very funny," I say and grab the rule book back.

"Looks like your Ma's first flower is coming up," she says. I look at the flowerpot where Bing Miller is buried and see a small bulb beginning to peek out from the dirt. *Thank you, Bing.*

The wall will go up in squares—thick metal posts raised to the sky, crossed by horizontal support beams. It's like a chessboard, with each square ready to be filled by green metal sheets. It will probably take weeks to complete, but it takes just one day for us to feel the barrier and see it take shape.

Home plate, third base, and right field will all be gone. I already miss the sliding catches, the players in the dugouts, the managers bickering, and the Jimmie Foxx home runs—only inches over the right-field wall. The sun, now on the other side of Shibe Park, is shining through the metal grid, creating strange shadows on the street below.

We barely talk, but we stay on the roof for hours. Lola rests her head on her knees as the men in hard hats pack up for the day, and the construction trucks sputter away. The street becomes eerily quiet.

"Let's not watch tomorrow," Lola finally says.

"Alright," I say. "Gosh, I have so much to tell you. About Ma and Pop and the store. And Nina's new job. About the church window and Connie Mack. Did you know that he donated the final $800 to help fix it? And Jimmie Foxx convinced him to do it? I've been parking cars and selling lemonade and making deliveries for Nick's Restaurant. And I have so many funny stories about it all." I stop to catch my breath.

She now has a grin from ear to ear.

"I missed you too," she says.

I rummage through my bag and hand Lola the journal.

"Here. I've been writing in it, but it's yours." She takes it, gingerly opening the bow and putting the ribbon into her hair. Her cheeks are flushed.

She opens the journal and looks closely at the photo I've taped to the inside cover, the one of us from the rooftop with Shibe Park in the background. Her eyes brighten, and her face fills with even more color.

She reads aloud what I've written underneath: *Rule #12: Jimmy and Lola will always be best friends forever.*

I watch as she flips to a blank page and titles her first entry: *Goodbye, Mr. Spalding.*

Epilogue

As long as the A's were in Florida, the weather was clear and hot and everything was serene.
—*The Sporting News*, April 11, 1934

"Run to the clubhouse and find me another pair of socks."

"Sure thing, Mr. Foxx!" I say, scurrying out of the dugout and into the ballpark hallway. Lola follows quickly behind, laughing as the A's newly adopted dog, Rags, nips at her heels. "Careful—Rags bit Dib Williams a couple of weeks ago, and he's still hurt."

"Going somewhere fast, I see." We both stop in our tracks at the sight of Connie Mack. Even after all of the events over the last few months, he's still the powerful manager of the A's. I still get a little nervous.

"Yes, sir. With all the rain, Mr. Foxx asked for a fresh pair of socks," I say.

Connie Mack bends down to pet Rags, who quickly runs away. He turns his focus to Lola. "The other Clubhouse Boys brought their fathers as guests to opening day."

251

Lola and I look at each other. We have been working on my *girls-should-be-allowed-in-the-dugout, too!* speech all morning.

"Yes, well," I clear my throat. "You remember Loughrea Sheridan? Lola?" I watch in relief as Connie Mack smiles.

"Of course." He turns to me. "Well done, Mr. Frances."

"Thank you, sir," I reply. No speech needed today.

"A girl in the dugout. I guess there is a first for everything," he says, and Lola lights up. Connie Mack shakes our hands and walks toward the field.

We are back just in time for the first at-bat. Even on this rainy, gray day, there is a buzz in the air. The players are chatting and laughing, telling jokes, and making snide remarks about the Washington players.

"So how do you like the view from here, Jimmy Frank?" Jimmie Foxx asks as the Senators take the field. I grin and look at Lola sitting next to me in the dugout.

"Not bad at all, Mr. Foxx," I reply.

"Today is my favorite day of the season," he says to us.

"Even in this rain?"

"You bet," he says and takes a deep breath. "Today is opening day."

"Rule #14," Lola and I say at the same time.

"I need to start writing these down. What's this one?" he asks as I hand him his bat.

"Rule #14: *On opening day, everyone is in first place.*"

Life's Little Rules

**(More Important Rules for
Jimmy & Lola's Eyes Only!)**

11. Watch every single Philadelphia Athletics home game from our rooftop, no matter what.
12. Jimmy and Lola will always be best friends forever.
13. Bury all dead family pets in Shibe Park for luck.
    Added: Flowerpots work, too.
    13a. Win lucky fish at every school fair.
14. On opening day, everyone is in first place.
15. Watch games from inside the ballpark on Knothole Gang days.
16. Always meet on the roof when you hear the Bingle.
17. A pinky promise cannot be broken.
18. Never eat cold pie.
19. Stay away from the four Polinski brothers at all costs.
    19a. Never be alone when the Polinskis are out to get you.

20. Keep fishing line, a matchbook, a library card, and a canteen on your person at all times.
21. Never say "I told you so."
22. Change the time of all doctor appointments when a shot is involved.
23. Take turns bringing snacks to Sunday games.
24. Eat lasagna off the floor whenever possible.
25. Create your own destiny.
26. Walls don't block us from the things that really matter.

Author's Note

Two fans watching the Philadelphia Athletics at Shibe Park

While many of the details within *Goodbye, Mr. Spalding* are historically accurate, this story is a work of fiction.

SO, WHAT IS TRUE?
Did the A's really play in Philadelphia? Who plays in Shibe Park today? Were there actually rooftop bleacher seats, and did the Spite Fence really exist?

THE PHILADELPHIA ATHLETICS
The Philadelphia Athletics played in the American League from 1901 through 1954. Early on, they established themselves as a strong team, and in their first thirty years, they won nine American League Pennants and five World

Series titles. Most sports historians include the 1929 A's among the most dominant teams in baseball history.

In 1955, the A's moved to Kansas City, Missouri, where they remained for thirteen years, and then they moved to Oakland, California, where they continue to play.

SHIBE PARK

Shibe Park, home of the Philadelphia Athletics, opened in 1909 and was the first baseball ballpark made from steel and reinforced concrete. *The Philadelphia Public Ledger* called it "a palace for fans," and many baseball

Shibe Park, Philadelphia—home of the Philadelphia Athletics, 1909–1954

historians point to Shibe Park as the start of a golden era for baseball stadiums. It was featured on the History Channel's *Modern Marvels*.

The Philadelphia Phillies made Shibe Park their home from 1938 through 1970, and the Philadelphia Eagles played home games there starting in 1940, until they moved to Franklin Field in 1958. Shibe Park was renamed Connie Mack Stadium in 1953 and hosted a variety of sporting events including all-star games, Negro League games, boxing, soccer, and rugby matches, among others.

Connie Mack Stadium was demolished in 1976.

Shibe Park grandstand entrance, before the 1914 World Series

THE BLEACHER SEATS & 20TH STREET COMMUNITY

The rooftop bleacher seats on 20th Street did exist and were a big part of the early Shibe Park experience. Home-owners sold seats, as well as space to radio broadcasters and television stations and for billboard advertisements. They also opened their third-floor windows to spectators. The bleachers were well organized and constructed, and a block committee was formed to help manage their efforts as a group.

Bruce Kuklick's 1993 book *To Every Thing a Season: Shibe Park and Urban Philadelphia 1909–1976* dives deep

Street view of the 20th Street rooftop bleachers during the 1929 Philadelphia Athletics season

into a neighborhood culture that thrived on baseball. For a personal account, John Rooney, a 20th Street resident, was interviewed in fall of 2009 for *Goodbye, Mr. Spalding* and provided a candid real-life glimpse of what it was like to be a young boy living across from Shibe Park. Mr. Rooney later published his own memoir in 2012, titled *Bleachers In the Bedroom: the Swampoodle Irish and Connie Mack*.

The neighborhood and ballpark attracted families and businesses from all areas. Some last names like Harvey, Carson, Polinski, and Kilroy were taken from historical references as surnames in the community, though all of the characters are fictional and do not resemble any living people. In addition, Doc Hoffman's, the Hop Inn, Reyburn Park, St. Columba, and some other locations frequented by Jimmy and Lola really did exist.

THE DEPRESSION ERA & THE SPITE FENCE

The Great Depression was a severe economic downturn during the 1930s. It was a time when jobs and food were scarce. It affected baseball, and by 1932, ballparks started to see a decrease in attendance.

At Shibe Park, the owners had never been happy with the "outlaw stands" across the street, and the declining attendance prompted them to take action. In March 1935, after much legal back-and-forth with the homeowners' association, the A's added 38 feet to the original 12-foot right-field wall. The rooftop seating that had once provided the neighborhood with substantial income now faced a green metal barrier, nicknamed the Spite Fence, which greatly affected the relationship between the team and the community.

Aerial view of the 20th Street rooftop bleachers during the 1929 World Series

CONNIE MACK

Connie Mack is the longest-serving team manager in baseball, serving as the A's manager from 1901 through 1950, and was elected to the National Baseball Hall of Fame in 1937. He was well known for creating several "dynasties," teams that brought great success to the A's and honor to the city of Philadelphia. These dynasties included players such as Eddie Collins, Jimmie Foxx, Mickey Cochrane, Al Simmons, Lefty Grove, and Bobby Shantz. He was equally well known for breaking up teams and selling off key players after championship seasons, giving the fans and sportswriters a lot of material to discuss and debate.

Philadelphia Athletics dugout, prior to start of game one, 1914 World Series at Shibe Park

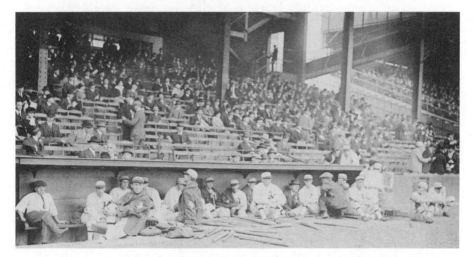

Mack was well liked among the baseball community, and he continued to be a respected fixture in the city of Philadelphia even after the team moved. He died in 1956, and during his funeral, all sixteen major league baseball team owners served as pallbearers. Today, his statue stands outside of Citizen's Bank Park, home of the Philadelphia Phillies.

THE SHIBES

Ben Shibe had a long history in baseball, starting in sporting goods and moving to team owner. He was president of the Philadelphia Athletics until his death in 1922, when his sons Tom and John Shibe took over as president and vice president, respectively.

John Shibe was in charge of all ballpark business and remodeling. According to Rich Westcott's book *Philadelphia's Old Ballparks*, John Shibe was the key voice spearheading efforts to build the Spite Fence. An avid sportsman, he was also known for having interests far beyond baseball, including working on his speedboats under the left-field stands.

JIMMIE FOXX

Jimmie Foxx was a three-time most valuable player and was inducted into the National Baseball Hall of Fame in 1951. He was a power hitter, ending his career with 534 home runs and a batting average of .325. He hit 30 or more home runs in 12 consecutive seasons, and in 1932, he hit a career-high 58 home runs, just two shy of tying the record. In 1935, the year the Spite Fence was built, he still managed to hit 36 home runs. Foxx was traded to the Boston Red Sox for the 1936 season.

During the fall of 1934, Babe Ruth, Lou Gehrig, Bing Miller, and Jimmie Foxx, among others, were led by Connie Mack on an all-star tour of Japan. On the way, they played exhibition games in Canada, where Jimmie

Foxx was knocked unconscious from a pitch by Barney "Lefty" Brown. He was released from the hospital after four days and continued the trip, hitting the longest home run of his career in Tokyo's Meiji Stadium only a short time later. Many historians point to this injury as the beginning of several future health problems.

Foxx had a good personality, and among the Clubhouse Boys, he was known for being the biggest tipper on the team. One of his favorite doubleheader meals was from Nick's on 22nd and Lehigh, where the Clubhouse Boys would run and buy him two Texas hot weiners for 15 cents.

Jimmie Foxx with Philadelphia Athletics' manager Connie Mack

RICHARDSON DILWORTH

The A's lawyer, Richardson Dilworth, successfully defended the Philadelphia Athletics both before and after the Spite Fence was built. Eventually, he began a career in politics, serving as Philadelphia's city treasurer and district attorney. He went on to be elected mayor of Philadelphia from 1956 to 1962. Dilworth Park, just outside of Philadelphia City Hall, is named in his memory.

THE SPALDING COMPANY AND BASEBALLS

The Spalding Company was the primary supplier of baseballs for the National League starting in 1876, and for both the National and American Leagues starting in 1889, when it acquired The Reach Company. To differentiate between the two leagues, Spalding continued to use the Reach name, and its trademark red and blue stitching, for American League balls. In 1934, both leagues started using all-red stitching.

In 1977, Rawlings won the baseball contract, and they continue to supply Major League Baseball today.

The phrase *Goodbye, Mr. Spalding* pays tribute to radio announcers of the past, who made calls like it with enthusiasm. It can be heard as delivered by a radio announcer in the 1984 movie *The Natural*.

THE A'S MASCOT: THE WHITE ELEPHANT

When the A's joined the American League in 1901, owner Ben Shibe was quick to offer large contracts to lure in star players. Giants' manager John McGraw, displeased with Shibe's actions, stated to reporters in 1902 that Shibe had a "big white elephant" on his hands.

The term, meant to describe something that looks great, but for which upkeep and care are impossible, was quickly picked up by an amused Connie Mack, who ordered all of the A's uniforms and gear to carry the white elephant. The symbol caught on and continues to be the Oakland A's mascot today.

MRS. CARSON'S GIFTS

Nina Allender was the official cartoonist of the National Woman's Party from 1914 until 1927. She drew hundreds of cartoons depicting the Suffragist Movement, seeking equal rights for women. The "Allender Girl" was a new image of Suffragists, showing them to be strong and independent women while being feminine at the same time.

The 1914 Baltimore News Babe Ruth rookie card is one of the rarest baseball cards in existence today. There are only ten known cards, which feature Ruth as an unknown minor league player. The card has come up for auction several times, with a sale in 2008 at the highest-ever purchase price of $517,000.

Resources

History and baseball have a strong and meaningful connection. Countless articles, websites, books, and museums are dedicated to chronicling our national pastime. Below are some of the resources used to help bring *Goodbye, Mr. Spalding* to life.

"Modern Marvels: Baseball Parks." Scheftel, Jeff, director. *Modern Marvels*, season 5, episode 15, The History Channel, 19 July 1999.

Philadelphia Bulletin, 1934–1935.

Philadelphia Inquirer, 1934–1935.

Daniel, Harrison W. *Jimmie Foxx: The Life and Times of a Baseball Hall of Famer, 1907–1967*. Jefferson, NC: McFarland, 1996.

Kashatus, William C. *The Philadelphia Athletics*. Charleston, SC: Arcadia, 2002.

Kuklick, Bruce. *To Every Thing a Season: Shibe Park and Urban Philadelphia, 1909–1976*. Princeton, NJ: Princeton University Press, 1991.

Lieb, Frederick G. *Connie Mack: Grand Old Man of Baseball.* New York: G.P. Putnam, 1945.

Mack, Connie. *My 66 Years in the Big Leagues; the Great Story of America's National Game.* Philadelphia: Winston, 1950.

Millikin, Mark R. *Jimmie Foxx: The Pride of Sudlersville.* Lanham, MD: Scarecrow, 1998.

Philadelphia Athletics Museum and Library, Hatboro, PA. [Now closed]

Rooney, John J. *Bleachers in the Bedroom: the Swampoodle Irish and Connie Mack.* Columbus OH: Zip Publishing/The Educational Publisher, 2012.

Shiffert, John. *Base Ball in Philadelphia: A History of the Early Game, 1831–1900.* Jefferson, NC: McFarland, 2006.

Sporting News (St. Louis, Missouri), 1934–1935. Archives: paperofrecord.com.

Warrington Bob. "John Shibe—A Biographic Sketch." *Philadelphia Athletics Historical Society*, October 26, 2005.

Westcott, Rich. *Philadelphia's Old Ballparks.*
Philadelphia: Temple University Press, 1996.

Temple University Urban Archives. George D. McDowell
Philadelphia Evening Bulletin Collection. Archival
photographs. Digital image. N.d.

Websites *

"An Ode to the Allender Girl." *Sewell-Belmont House &
Museum.* October 19, 2011. nationalwomansparty.
org/an-ode-to-the-allender-girl/.

National Baseball Hall of Fame. baseballhall.org.

Websites active at time of publication.

Acknowledgments

I have an amazing family who encouraged and supported me every step of the way. Thank you to my husband Tom, and daughters Katelyn and Olivia. You are the three most lovable and fun people I know. Thanks for rooting for me, and Jimmy and Lola, all of these years!

Thanks to my mother, Lucille, who really is the best storyteller, and whose family stories found their way into several parts of this book. Thanks to my father, Stan, my sister Michele and family—John, Austin, Matt, Amanda—and all of my extended family and friends for their continued support.

For over eight years, I have worked on *Goodbye, Mr. Spalding*. Writing partners Eileen Ruvane, Hallee Adelman, and Tammy Higgins were with me from the beginning, encouraging and challenging my progress every step along the way. Thanks to Uncle Jethro and our Imaginary-But-Real writing conferences, which kicked me in gear every year. I don't think there is a way to show you just how grateful I am for your friendship! I could not ask for a more supportive or smarter team.

Thank you to my editor Carolyn Yoder, who saw something in this idea from the start. It was June 2010 when I attended her historical fiction intensive workshop with only the idea for this book in mind, and it's hard to believe that *Goodbye, Mr. Spalding* found its home with Calkins Creek seven years later. Thanks to Brittany Ryan, Lori Lyons, Juanita Galuska, Barbara Grzeslo, Barbara Skalak, and everyone in the Boyds Mills Press and Highlights family for believing in me!

Thank you to my agent, Tracy Marchini, whose passion for history makes writing for children so much fun. You are enthusiastic and approachable, and I appreciate you as an agent, editor, and friend. Thanks also to the behind-the-scenes and diligent team at BookEnds Literary Agency, especially Jessica Faust, James McGowan, Jean Marie Pierson, and Beth Campbell.

Thank you to all the people—editors, agents, peers—who have helped shape *Goodbye, Mr. Spalding* over the years. Thanks especially to authors Wendy Mass, Lynda Mullaly Hunt, Kat Yeh, Donna Gephart, and Kim Savage for sound advice along the way.

The Society of Children's Book Writers and Illustrators (SCBWI) Pocono Retreats in eastern Pennsylvania were a difference maker, and critical to the development of *Goodbye, Mr. Spalding*. Conferences with the Rutgers University Council on Children's Literature (RUCCL) had a similar impact. Writers: join these groups! They are wonderful for support and guidance in creating children's literature.

Thanks to baseball historian and University of Pennsylvania Professor of American History Emeritus Dr. Bruce Kuklick for reading and evaluating my work with such enthusiasm. Thanks also to Dr. John Rooney, a former resident of 20th Street who was interviewed in his offices at La Salle University. I am grateful to have experts willing to share knowledge and advice.

I would like to especially thank the Philadelphia sports community. Over the years, I have connected with speakers at the Free Library of Philadelphia, workers at the former Philadelphia Athletics Museum, and baseball historians. Most of all, I have met countless A's and Phillies fans who have fond memories of Shibe Park and Connie Mack Stadium, all of whom have been eager to share their stories. The A's are still going strong in Oakland, and I am happy to help keep their rich Philadelphia history alive.

Text and Picture Credits

Thanks especially to the Temple University Urban Archives, the family of photographer Leslie Jones, and the Library of Congress. Thanks also to Jim Penegar for access to headlines and quotes from *The Sporting News*. All rights reserved. Reprinted with permission.

Library of Congress, Prints & Photographs Division:
    LC-USZ62-79895: 256; LC-DIG-ggbain-17517:
    257; LC-DIG-ggbain-17523: 261

Special Collections Research Center, Temple University
    Libraries, Philadelphia, PA: 255, 258, 260

Courtesy of the Boston Public Library, Leslie Jones
    Collection: 263.